carry her heart

ALSO BY HOLLY JACOBS

Just One Thing

Christmas in Cupid Falls

carry her heart

HOLLY JACOBS

Montlake
Romance

Text copyright © 2015 Holly Jacobs

Published by Montlake Romance, Seattle

www.apub.com

Amazon, the Amazon logo, and Montlake Romance are trademarks of Amazon.com, Inc., or its affiliates.

ISBN-13: 9781477829288
ISBN-10: 1477829288

Cover design by Mumtaz Mustafa

Library of Congress Control Number: 2014958167

Printed in the United States of America

To Abbey: This one's for you!

Freshman Year

Chapter One

I sat on my front porch and took a sip from a bone china teacup with tiny forget-me-nots painted on the side.

It was a civilized, proper cup.

I looked down at my laptop, which was balanced on the holey jeans that covered my outstretched legs. My legs were propped on the porch railing.

There was nothing particularly proper looking about me.

I didn't need a mirror to know that my carrot-red hair had gone Medusa again and was breaking free of its twisty. As for my jeans, I swear my knees must be knobbier than the average woman's, or maybe because I worked at home and wore them daily, they just gave up more rapidly. Either way, my three favorite pairs of jeans all had holes in the knees . . . again.

I'd have to go shopping.

I hate going shopping.

I could buy most of what I needed online and avoid the stores, but jeans were an item of clothing that must be tried on.

I stared at my blank screen and took another sip of my tea.

I liked working on the porch.

I watched all the cars that stopped in front of the school across the street. Passenger doors opened and children were disgorged from them at regular intervals. Tall, skinny kids, short, roundish ones. Loud ones who started shrieking friends' names before their feet hit the pavement. Quiet ones, who could seem alone even in the midst of the morning chaos.

Boys. Girls. Nerds. Jocks. Happy. Sullen.

They were all my inspiration.

They were also my audience.

In a sea of young adult books that dealt with paranormal elements, from wizards to vampires, I currently wrote reality-based books for pre-teens. I'd written books for much younger children in the past, but as my audience aged, so did my writing.

Maybe it was time to think about writing for high school students rather than for middle school?

I tried to concentrate on the scene in front of me. I only had a few more weeks before the Erie, Pennsylvania, weather got too cold to work outside. I always hated moving inside for work. This porch was where I found *Julie and Auggie, Terry the Terrible,* and *Beautiful Belle.*

This porch was also where I tried to imagine Amanda.

There.

A girl with auburn-brown braids that thumped up and down on her back as she walked to a group of girls and joined in the talk. She was new. I know I'd have remembered her. She was talking to a group of bigger kids. Probably eighth graders, the oldest class at this school. She was animated as she spoke. She'd work as a character. I . . .

I was distracted from the scene playing out across the street by a moving van that pulled into the driveway next door. The Morrisons had moved out three weeks ago. The *"For Sale"* sign on the front yard had had a *"Sold"* sticker plastered across it for a few weeks longer than that. But after the Morrisons had moved out, no one else had moved in.

The door of the van opened and a man got out.

I only needed that first quick glance to know he was cute.

I tried to study him circumspectly. And I immediately thought of him as a fictional character. If I were writing him in a book, I'd make him a . . . coach. He had that *every-man* sort of look to him. He was good-looking, but not intimidatingly so. Still, he was good-looking enough that there was a spark of attraction.

I'll confess, I don't go out a lot and don't meet a ton of eligible, single men. I meet even fewer who give me that zing of awareness. The sort of feeling that reminded me that I was a woman in my prime.

I took another glance at the man I was zinging over. His hair was . . . neat. Not too short but not long by any stretch of the imagination. And it was brown. Not dark brown bordering on black and definitely not punctuated with blond highlights. No, this man's hair was a straight-up, use-a-Crayola-brown-crayon-if-you-were-coloring-him sort of brown.

He was tan. Not in a lies-out-in-the-sun sort of way, but rather he had a skin tone that came from ancestors who came from sunnier climates than mine. I made people who were pale look swarthy.

Judging from the van, he was not overly tall, nor was he overly short. Average.

I tried to ignore my zing and concentrate on my book. This man would make a perfect coach. Put a baseball cap on him and give him a whistle and a glove . . .

At some point, I'd started typing.

"Couch," Felicity called. "Your name's funny."

"Coach," Coach Divan responded, correcting her pronunciation.

"Couch Divan. I bet people pick on you. My grandma calls her couch a divan. So you're really Couch Couch."

"Coach," he repeated.

"I like Couch better. Couch Divan. Yep. Couch Couch. Yeah, I like it—"

"Hi."

That one syllable pulled me from my story and I realized the man who had reminded me I was a woman and was my potential new neighbor as well as an inspiration for a new character was standing at my porch railing.

"Sorry. I got caught up in . . ." I wasn't going to tell him what I'd been caught up in. It's better not to scare new acquaintances with my profession. Some worry they'd become fodder for my fiction.

Frankly, some did.

I started again. "Hi. Are you my new neighbor?"

He nodded. "Edward Chesterfield. Ned, to my friends."

I couldn't help it. I started to laugh. Really, it was more of a giggle than a full-out laugh.

I'd written an article years ago for a historical magazine about the evolution of the modern sofa, which was the only reason I know that a variety of couches are known as *Chesterfields*.

Given what I'd been writing, it was funny. Well, maybe not in a stand-up comedy routine sort of way, but to a woman who spent a lot of her time entertaining herself, it was hysterical.

My new neighbor, Ned, looked at me like I was nuts.

"Sorry. Really. It's just that . . ." Man, I was making a muck of this. I'm pretty sure that telling a man you were amused that there was a type of couch that bore his family name wasn't going to convince him of your sanity.

I settled for simply introducing myself. "I'm Piper. Piper George. Do you need a hand moving stuff in?"

"Miss Pip," a group of kids from last year called from across the street. I was the kindergarten story lady at the school. Some years, for first or second grade, too. I went in a few times a week. Sometimes I read *my* books, and sometimes I simply read some of my favorite children's books. *Where the Wild Things Are, The Wild Baby Book* . . .

I waved back to the kids. "Have a good first day."

"Pip?" my new neighbor asked.

That was my writing name and how the kids all knew me, but no adults called me that. "It's Piper," I corrected. "So do you need any help, Ned?"

He shook his head. "Thanks, but I have some friends coming over to help."

"Well, good luck and welcome to the neighborhood. If you need anything, I'm around more often than I'm not." Great. Now he was convinced I was nuts and a hermit. So I added an explanation. "I work from home."

He nodded and asked, "Are you going to explain what's so funny about my name?"

I smiled. "It wasn't your name, but my mind."

"Your mind, Pip?" he asked.

"Piper," I corrected again. "And my mind works in mysterious ways, Ned Chesterfield."

He studied me a moment, then simply nodded and went back to his driveway.

I was pretty sure I had not made an auspicious first impression.

But seriously, my inspiration for *Couch* Divan—Couch Couch— was a Chesterfield?

I chuckled again.

Little things amused me. That was a good thing, because little things were far more prevalent in my life than big things. Some people might have a problem with that, but frankly, I loved my life. I made a living at my writing, which allowed me to spend my free time volunteering. I thought both things made a difference, and that was enough for me.

I took a sip of my now-cold tea from my favorite forget-me-not cup and went back to work on *Couch Couch*. I watched as a car full of men pulled up next door and began unloading the moving van with Ned Chesterfield.

They all waved and said *hi*, or at least nodded.

I couldn't wait to tell my friend Cooper that the new neighbor was cute. Or maybe I wouldn't. If she found out he was good-looking she'd go out of her way to fix the two of us up. I might try to tell her that I had more requirements from the men I dated other than being cute, but she would insist that the first spark of attraction was all I needed to date. Later, I could find out if there was more.

I watched as Ned came in and out of the house.

And yes, if Coop asked, I'd have to admit there was a spark.

After an hour or so, another car pulled up and parked in front of my house, under my serviceberry tree this time. A pretty blonde got out carrying a big bag. She was tiny. The term *sprite* came to mind. Yes, if I were writing her in a book, I'd write her as a sprite. She smiled and nodded at me. I smiled back.

My new neighbor came out and saw her walking toward his new house. "Mela."

It was an odd name, but she smiled as he said it. They hugged. Not a PDA sort of uncomfortable embrace but just a friendly hug. If I were writing them in a book, they'd be a couple who didn't make it. They didn't really seem to . . . *fit*.

I have no idea what *fit* really means in terms of a relationship, but some people just do. My parents, for instance. I can't imagine one without the other, and not simply because they're my parents, but because they . . . well, *fit*.

Ned and this Mela didn't seem to.

"I came to give your new man cave a woman's touch," she announced.

He laughed. "John is already setting up the sixty-inch flat-screen television in the living room, so basically, the house is pretty much ready to go. No touches required."

She laughed and held up her bag. "I brought candles. Girly-smelling candles."

"Heaven save me from smelly candles," he said with a smile.

They continued teasing about televisions, candles, and a woman's touch.

My new neighbor had a girlfriend.

I thought there was a very good chance I was going to like Ned Chesterfield, but I quickly snuffed out that initial jolt. He was taken. It was almost a relief. I'd never have to worry about dating someone next door. I mean, how awkward would it be if we dated and then broke up?

I was definitely relieved he had a girlfriend.

⚕ ⚕ ⚕

That night, as I locked up the house, I saw light spilling from the windows next door. It seemed that my new neighbor was all moved in and was spending his first night there.

I wondered if he was still unpacking, or if indeed his big television was all he needed to feel at home.

I knew if I moved, I'd require more than that to feel settled.

I made my way upstairs to my bedroom. It occupied the entire second-floor dormer of my house. I flipped on the light and realized it felt like home. I studied it as if for the first time.

It contained a weird mix of family antiques and thrift-store finds. My great aunt's bird's-eye maple-and-mahogany vanity stood between two old chests of drawers I'd picked up at a garage sale and painted a turquoise blue, which complemented my most treasured family antique—the wedding chest under the window.

My bedframe was a flea-market find. I think I'd paid ten dollars for it. It was cast iron and had been painted once upon a time, but now only held a ghost of that white paint, mixed with the metal and a bit of rust. The woman had said with a good sanding and a coat of paint it would look like new. I didn't do either because I liked the air of age on it. It was covered with an antique forget-me-not quilt I'd picked up at a house sale last year.

Yes, the things in this room felt like home. A simple television wouldn't do it. Nor would scented candles.

Almost every piece of furniture in this room had a story, and those stories were part of what made it—and my entire house—feel like home.

Thinking about stories and home, I climbed in bed, opened my nightstand drawer, and took out the journal I'd bought a few weeks ago. Its cover was a soft leather that whispered it was antique, even though it wasn't.

The first time I'd opened it and inhaled, I swear the smell said, *Write in me. Fill me with letters, adding one to another until you have a word. Then stack those words and turn them into colors and textures. Turn those into feelings and joy. Turn them into a story. Not one of your normal stories, those broad-brush strokes that paint the pictures that parade through your mind. Turn this into Amanda's story.*

String those words together and paint her story. Tell her about all the good she's done, even if she hasn't been aware of it.

I opened that leather journal now and the spine crackled softly. And as I stared at that first blank page, I knew it was time.

Amanda was starting high school. She was standing on the brink of adulthood. Someday soon she might come and find me, and when she did, I had so much to share with her. So much I wanted to be sure she understood.

I looked at that wedding trunk that had once been a bright blue with red flowers hand-painted on it. Both colors had faded over time. I knew that the letters on the front were faded as well, but still discernable. T. P. E. 1837.

My mother said she thought it came from Sweden with a bunch-of-greats-grandmother, Talia Piper Eliason. Mom had given it to me when I moved out, but I never felt as if I owned it. I was holding it for Amanda. Like the locket I'd sent with her, this was her family history.

I knew that Amanda had a new name and a new family. She had a story she'd grown up knowing. But she couldn't understand the entirety of her life until I told her this part.

When I'd bought the journal, I'd thought I'd tell her story chron-
ologically, but I wasn't ready to talk about her birth, so I started at
another point . . .

Dear Amanda,

*Amanda's Pantry truly began on your fifth birthday,
almost a decade ago now. I was at the grocery store buying . . . I don't remember what I was buying. Probably
something with no nutritional value whatsoever. I was
only twenty-one, and I didn't worry about things like
proper nutrition.*

*I was standing in line at the register behind a young
woman and a toddler. The little girl had red hair. Not
auburn. Not strawberry blond. Red. Like Orphan Annie
red. Like mine. I felt a kinship with her immediately,
and of course, I thought of you.*

*She was asking for a piece of candy and her mom
was whispering, "No." There was something in the way
her mom said it that told me that she wasn't saying no
because it was candy and the little girl shouldn't be eating
candy. She was saying no because she couldn't afford it.*

*I was about to buy the candy bar and then run it
out to them after I paid, when the cashier said, "That's
twenty-eight o' six." I remember the amount, even if I
don't remember what was in my cart.*

The woman had a twenty in her hand.

"I think we can do without—"

*I wasn't sure what she'd be able to do without. The
bread? The peanut butter? Or maybe the milk?*

*And at that moment, I looked at that little girl who
could have been you. And I thought, what if she was you?*

What if your father lost his job? What if your mother got sick?

God forbid, what if you got sick?

What if you were standing in the grocery store, hungry while your mom decided what food you could do without?

I looked at the redheaded toddler and felt tears well up in my eyes.

And I realized my hand was already in my back pocket. Before her mother could put anything back, I bent over and came up with a ten-dollar bill in my hand. "Ma'am, I think you dropped this," I said.

She gave me a small smile and shook her head. "No, I didn't, but thank you."

"Ma'am, I saw it fly out of your purse. Really. Here." I thrust the ten-dollar bill at her.

And she looked at me and I knew that she knew what I was doing. I saw the tears in her eyes. She knew I was lying in order to preserve her dignity and she allowed me that fib.

"Thank you," she whispered.

She paid for the food, the clerk bagged the items, and the woman took her daughter and the bags and then walked toward the door. Like I said, I don't know what I had on the checkout belt, but I quickly pulled the candy bar off the shelf, added it to my purchases, paid, and ran to catch the lady. "May I?" I asked, letting the mom catch a glimpse of the candy bar.

She nodded. I knelt down to the little girl, who was clutching her mother's hand. "Here you go. Maybe if you eat a good supper tonight, you can have this for dessert."

The little girl's eyes bugged out a little and she mutely nodded.

"Why?" the mom asked as I rose.

"For Amanda," was my reply.

I could see that she didn't understand, but that didn't matter. I did. And I felt more at peace than I had in a long time.

"I can't repay you," she said.

"Don't worry about it. Someday when things get easier, you can pass it on."

She nodded. "I will. And I'll tell Jean about it someday."

"No. You don't have to tell her, or anyone. Really."

And I walked away.

I had the nightmare again that night. You were cold and hungry and I couldn't get to you. I ripped apart my pantry and couldn't find anything for you to eat. But you came into my kitchen, sat down at the counter, and picked up a candy bar that was suddenly lying there.

You looked at me and said, "Thank you," as you pushed a strand of your carrot-colored hair behind your ear and then tore into the candy.

Love,
Piper

Chapter Two

I met my best friend my first day of college. None of my high school friends were going to Gannon University, so the school assigned me a roommate my freshman year. Julie Cooper.

When I walked into my dorm room my freshman year, Coop was already there. Despite the fact she was standing on her bed, I could tell she was tiny. She had dark, wildly curly hair and a beautiful copper complexion.

I noticed those three attributes right away because they were so opposite of mine. I was on the taller side of things, with very red hair, and I was so pale that I used to swear the glare from my legs could blind drivers.

My new roommate was on her bed hanging a poster . . . a map of Middle Earth.

Despite our physical differences, when I looked at that map, I knew we were going to be friends.

We roomed together all four years of college.

I quizzed Coop on English classics and she quizzed me on human anatomy. We tried the college party scene together and discovered that we didn't like it. We dated twin brothers our sophomore year of college, then dumped them within a week of each other.

We bonded over those first loves and breakups, just as we bonded over the good teachers and bad ones. We shared a love for Tolkien, ice cream, and trivia.

And we'd stayed friends since that first day.

Coop taught middle school English for the school district and we tried to get together at least once a month for a girls' night.

Now for some single women, girls' night might mean hitting a bar or a club, or at least a restaurant, but for me and Coop, girls' night meant a pizza at the picnic table in the backyard and a wild game of rummy. I mean, we didn't play Five Hundred Rummy. No, we were truly *wild* and played One Thousand Rummy.

And sometimes, if the mood struck and we were seriously crazed, we'd try for Two Thousand Rummy.

Tonight, I'd started a fire in my fire pit for warmth. I realized this was probably our last outdoor girls' night until next season. Next month, we'd have to move inside.

My picnic table and fire pit were located between the house and the rest of my crazy garden. Tonight, the garden was louder than it had been during the summer. The apple tree leaves still clung to their branches and made the slightest crinkly sound in the breeze. The lemon balm just beyond the picnic table had grown to immense size this summer, and now that it had dried it had a deeper crackle that seemed to harmonize with the apple leaves. Both were punctuated by the occasional snap of the fire. Each breath of wind seemed to intensify the sound, as if it was conducting a song that only the garden knew.

As soon as Coop arrived, I forgot my garden's song. Our games of rummy could get quite loud. Coop slapped down her cards with a screech of victory. "Ha. Another hand for me. Count 'em up."

I mock-grumbled, which was expected in one of our marathon games. There was no losing with grace. No, because we were so wild, we both groused and taunted at will. "It's a good thing we're playing to a thousand instead of five hundred. Otherwise—"

Coop interrupted and finished my sentence. "—otherwise, this game would be over in record time."

I saw my new neighbor's face pop up over the fence. "Is everything okay, Piper?"

He'd only lived next door a few weeks, but I was right the first day; he seemed like a good neighbor. He took me at my word and came to the door his second week and asked for a cup of sugar. It was such a stereotypical neighbor thing that I laughed as he held the cup out, but this time he got the joke and laughed with me.

"Ned, come over," I called. "I want to introduce you to my friend."

"Her *best* friend," Coop qualified loudly.

"My best friend," I corrected.

Moments later, Ned opened the gate that stood between our two houses and came into my backyard for the first time.

"Wow," he said.

I looked around and realized that even in the firelight, it was easy to see how crowded my backyard was.

"I can see the treetops from my upstairs window, so I knew you had . . . a lot going on back here, but it's different from this perspective."

I laughed. As a writer, I'd long since realized that *perspective* was everything. "It gets a little more wild every year," I told him. Then I made the introduction. "Ned, this is my friend Julie Cooper."

"Call me Cooper," Coop, who hated the name Julie, said as she extended her hand.

"Edward Chesterfield," he said as he shook it. "Ned."

Coop gave a little snort, and I knew she was thinking about Couch Couch. I shouldn't have shared that particular new character with her, and I definitely shouldn't have told her where I got the inspiration.

But she didn't say anything about that, she just said, "There's a lot of pizza and room at the card table if you're interested."

"What are we playing?" he asked, eyeing the pile of cards in the middle of the picnic table. "Five-card stud or—"

"Five Hundred Rummy," Coop said.

"Only, we are as wild as my backyard and added another five hundred, so we're playing One Thousand Rummy," I corrected. "Yeah, I know, you're shocked by our utter disregard for the rules."

Ned grinned. "I am definitely shocked. Deal me in." He helped himself to a slice of pizza as he sat down.

We played for an hour—I was winning—before Mela called Ned from the back door.

"I'm over at Pip's," he called back. "Why don't you come over?"

"Okay," she said, but even Cooper could hear her lack of enthusiasm, because she gave me a look that said, *What's up with her?* I shrugged to indicate I didn't have a clue.

Ned had introduced us a few days after he moved in, and I made it a point to wave to her when she came in or out of Ned's, but unless he was around, she managed to look right through me. She turned me invisible this time, too, as she came into the backyard and smiled only at Ned. "I got worried when I couldn't find you," she said.

"Sorry. I forgot you were coming over. We were playing cards."

Ned forgetting she was coming over didn't seem to please Mela at all.

I tried to pretend I didn't notice that not only was she annoyed with him, she'd managed to turn both me *and* Coop invisible.

Houdini had nothing on Mela.

I said, "Hi, Mela. I don't think you've met my friend, Coop."

For a moment, we were visible as she responded, "It's a pleasure," in such a way that it was apparent it wasn't a pleasure at all. Then she promptly turned us invisible again and said, "Ned, I brought that movie we were going to watch."

"You're welcome to join our game of rummy," Coop offered. "And I think Ned might have left a slice of pizza if you're hungry."

Mela shook her head. "It's been a long week. I just want to sit down, watch a movie, and relax with my *boyfriend*." She put a heavy emphasis on the word *boyfriend*, just to stake her claim, I think.

"Sure, hon," Ned said. "Thanks for the game, ladies."

"Any time," I said.

Mela didn't so much as touch Ned, but it felt as if she were dragging him out of the backyard.

After we heard his back door slam shut, Coop whispered, "I feel like I'm ten again, and a friend's mom just took him home because it was bedtime."

I laughed, then grew serious as I confessed, "She doesn't like me."

"I'm expecting you to be nominated for sainthood any day now. I like you and I've got impeccable taste. How can anyone else not like you?" Coop asked.

"The world is full of mysteries," I joked, though the fact that Mela disliked me and I couldn't think of anything I'd done to her in the few short weeks I'd known her, bothered me. "Plus, I don't think that's how sainthood works, and I'm absolutely sure, however it works, I'm not on the nominating committee's list."

I was lucky to have Coop in my life. Everyone should have a friend who only sees the best in him or her. A friend who never notices the flaws, or if she does notice, simply ignores them.

I had Coop, so I didn't need Mela to be my new best friend, but I'd tried to be pleasant. If Ned and I were chatting when she came over, I always tried to include her in the conversation.

She didn't want to be included.

Did I remind her of her mean sister?

Was there a redheaded girl in grade school who'd beat her out for the lead role in the Thanksgiving play?

What if she'd lost her last boyfriend and a part in the play to a redhead?

And then what if . . .

Ideas flitted in and out of my mind the rest of the evening. When Coop left, I jotted a few of the better what-ifs down as fodder for future stories, then took the journal into the backyard and pulled a chair near the dying embers of the fire and wrote my second message to Amanda.

Dear Amanda,

I think maybe I was always destined to be a writer because what-if has always been a question I've been willing to ask myself.

I need you to understand that I asked it throughout my entire pregnancy:

What if I kept you?

What if I gave you up for adoption?

I played scenario after scenario in my head.

What if I kept you, but couldn't make it through college with a baby, so I continued working at my high school job at the restaurant? We could barely make it on my salary, so we lived in a less-than-desirable section of town, and then you joined a gang . . .

Or what if I kept you and did manage to go to college as a young single mom, but my classes took so much time away from you that you never felt loved?

And then what if . . .

I couldn't see a way to keep you and give you the kind of childhood I'd had. One with a mother and father who might not be rich, but who lived comfortably. I wanted you to have a mother who would read you a book at night, not be sitting at a desk doing her own homework. I wanted to give you a father who would believe you were the best, the brightest, and the most marvelous being he'd ever met.

I kept playing what-if-I-kept-you scenarios, but at the end of each, I could hear the biggest what-if of all. It was the one I couldn't shake.

What if I was as strong as my great-grandmother had been and gave you the gift of the type of childhood I'd had by sending you into the arms of someone else? What if I gave you to parents who longed for a child and had the time, experience, and the income to give you a child-hood like mine?

What if I was as strong as my great-grandmother Rose? My parents have given me her name as a middle name. Piper Rose George.

She was my grandfather's mom and he'd told me her story countless times when I was younger. He'd told it to me so often that it felt like it was as much my story as his and hers.

Grandpa used to say I was the spitting image of his mother. "Her hair was as red as a cherry tomato," he'd tell me.

My great-grandmother Rose grew up in an Irish family with too many children and too little money. She married my great-grandfather when she was only sixteen. He was a blacksmith and made a comfortable living. They had my grandfather and seemed to be on the road to a happily-ever-after. But when their baby—my grand-father—was only two months old, his father was kicked in the head by a horse and died two days later.

Rose went to work in a hotel as a maid to sup-port herself and my grandfather. Grandpa was shuffled around from one set of relatives to another.

When he was five, Rose made a decision to give him up in order for him to have a better life. The life she'd dreamed for him.

I've imagined how hard it must have been to put her five-year-old son on a ship to America. To send him to live with an older sister my great-grandmother hardly remembered. An older sister, Nettie, who'd never married and told Rose in her letters that she longed for a child . . . not a husband, just a child.

Rose wanted her son to have the best. In addition to longing for a child, her sister worked at a school. Nettie promised Rose my grandfather would have the best education, and she would raise him and love him as if he were her own son.

So Rose sent Grandpa on that ship to a country she'd never seen and a sister she didn't remember and only knew through letters.

I stood up and set the journal down on my chair. The deep reds and orange of the embers were fading and I was once again aware of the music of my garden. It sounded like a whisper.

I'd pictured Rose sending my grandfather away so many times when I was pregnant, and I'd marveled at her strength. I wanted to be as strong as she'd been.

I sat back down and picked up the journal.

I imagined that scene a hundred times. A busy dock in front of a huge ship. In my mind, it looked like the Brig Niagara—the famous ship from the Battle of Lake Erie. Its replica was present-day Erie's pride and joy. I know that the ship my grandfather took would have been more modern than that, but still, I saw the Niagara when I pictured the scene.

I could see Rose kneeling next to Grandpa, hugging him to her. Kissing his forehead. Trying to make him know to his core that even though she was sending him away, he was loved.

In my mind's eye, she took her locket from around her neck and slipped it around his. My grandfather had left me that locket when he passed away. Inside was a picture of Rose and her blacksmith husband.

Rose sent it across an ocean with my grandfather, wanting to be sure he never forgot where he came from.

Needing to know he would never forget he was loved.

Rose continued to work at the hotel. Every month she sent Nettie money for Grandpa's care. But she never managed to save any for her own passage to America.

Rose died twelve years later when Grandpa was seventeen.

She never knew that her dreams for him came to fruition. My grandfather loved his Aunt Nettie. He also loved books and went to college. He became a teacher.

I believe Rose would have been so proud, knowing her sacrifices gave him a good life.

Amanda, the question I kept coming back to throughout my pregnancy was, could I be as strong as Rose had been? Could I put your needs first?

All those times I asked myself what if I kept you, I never found a scenario where you'd have the childhood I wanted for you. My parents had offered to help me, but even with their help, I was afraid I'd shortchange you.

But what if I gave you up, like Rose? When I asked myself that question, I could picture so many scenarios in which you had a wonderful, happy childhood and grew into an amazing young woman.

What would be best for you?

I knew the answer the first time I asked myself that question.

And on that August day, I held you for an hour and, like Rose, I hugged you and sent you into someone else's care. I gave you to your parents. I called out, 'Goodbye, Amanda,' as they took you home to a better life than I could have given you.

A life that wouldn't include me.

And as I cried, I knew just how hard Rose's decision must have been. I'd loved you for nine months and held you for one hour. Rose had loved and held my grandfather for five years.

I gave the adoption agency a letter for you. I hope your parents gave it to you when they felt you were old enough.

I put Rose's locket inside the envelope, hoping you'd realize that, like Rose, I loved you enough to send you away.

I hoped you'd know that you were loved.

Are loved.

Love,
Piper Rose

Sophomore Year

Chapter Three

Another first day of school. It was hot for a school day. I was barefoot and wearing shorts and an old *Les Mis* T-shirt. I was drinking iced tea rather than hot tea.

I'd spent most of my day on the porch working. But the words had dried up a while ago. I'd been just going through the motions.

I glanced at the journal that was on the table next to me. I knew what I was going to write *today*.

> *Dear Amanda,*
>
> *It's another first day of school here. This morning I sat on the front porch and watched all the students across the street arrive, ready to start the school year. It was such a hot summer, and summer wasn't ready to release its grip on Erie just because it was the first day of school.*
>
> *There were some familiar faces in the swarm of children. They waved and called out "good-mornings," or "hey-Ms.-Pips." And as always there are new ones— kindergarteners and older transfer students.*

As I write to you, it's almost time for the dismissal bell. I know the children will all rush out, their first day over.

Only one hundred and seventy-nine more to go.

You're a sophomore this year. You'll hopefully be returning to the same school as last year. You'll be greeting old friends and going to those first classes and discovering what they will be like this year.

I always loved the first day of school. There's such a sense of possibility about it. Anything can happen.

I adored when the teachers handed out textbooks. When I was lucky, it was a brand-new one. I loved the creeeeek sound the binding made when you opened it for the first time. I loved the smell. I loved writing my name in the box—the first one to proclaim I used that particular book and the years I used it.

Years.

I sat the journal on my lap and looked at the school across the street. Amanda had had ten first days of school.

No, eleven if you counted kindergarten.

More if she'd gone to preschool.

I wondered if she liked school. I hoped so.

I felt a wave of nostalgia for the moments that I'd never experienced with her and for all the talks we'd never had.

I picked up the journal again. It was my opportunity to talk to Amanda. Maybe it was a one-way conversation, but that made it easier in a way.

So many have passed since I held you. I knew you for only nine months, held you for one short hour, and yet I've built my life around you.

So what story should I start the school year off with?

I haven't told you about what I do.

I don't do what I thought I'd do. Maybe that's a lesson for you. Choose a path, but don't be afraid to change directions.

You see, I went to college to be a nurse.

And at first, I thought I'd work L&D . . . labor and delivery. But I did an externship on the pediatric floor and loved it. That's where I worked after I graduated. For a while, I thought I'd spend my life working there.

My mother believed I was punishing myself for giving you up by working with children on a daily basis. But that wasn't it at all. I never felt I needed to be punished for giving you a better life. I truly believed then— and now—that giving you to a family who was better equipped to care of you was an act of love. Like Grandmother Rose—it was my gift to you. I gave you a family who could give you the life I wanted for you but couldn't have given you myself.

No, working with children wasn't me punishing myself. It was my solace. Every time I comforted a crying baby, I comforted you. Every time I held a sick, lonely child, I held you.

You led me to nursing, and nursing led me to my real passion—telling stories.

How? I'd been working on the pediatric floor for about two years, and I had a five-year-old patient who visited our unit frequently. I can't tell you her name or why she was a regular because of patient confidentiality, but she was precocious and most days she meandered somewhere between a delight and a holy terror.

One night she asked me, "Miss Piper, do you have a little girl?"

I felt as if the earth had stopped spinning for a moment. Everything seemed to come to a screeching halt. Everything around me was perfectly still. I was immobile. I thought my heart had stopped beating at the reminder of what I'd lost.

No, not lost. What I'd willingly given away.

Then slowly, I felt my heart begin to beat again. Its first thump filled my ears to the point of being almost deafening.

But slowly, I reacquainted myself with the sound of my heartbeats, and the earth started spinning as well. Still, I didn't know how to answer this simplest of questions. So I asked her a question instead. "Why, honey?"

"'Cause you'd be a good mom."

This time I was ready for the pain. I was braced. The world and my heart continued their rhythms as I let that innocent comment rip through me.

"Thank you." She'd wounded me, tearing loose the scab on my heart. No matter how many times I thought I'd thoroughly healed, the scab always ended up ripped away by sometimes the smallest actions or words.

Still, her compliment helped staunch the bleeding from the now-open wound. Like I said, I believed giving you up was indeed the mark of a good mom, but that never stopped me from missing you. From hurting.

"Can you tell me a story?" she asked, not noticing my pain.

My shift was almost over, so I nodded. "Let me go find Nurse Abbey and then I'll come back and bring a book."

She shook her head. "No, not a book story. One from your head."

I came back ten minutes later with a book in hand, despite her decree. "This is a very good story—" I started.

She shook her head again and reiterated, "No, from your head. Those are the best kinds of stories," she added, as if anyone with any sense should know that.

She gave me a look that said only the best would be good enough for her.

Bowing to the inevitable, I said, "There was a—"

"No. Stories start with Once Upon a Time.*"*

"Once Upon a Time there was a girl named," I tried to think of a name, and from nowhere, I found one. "Belinda Mae Abernathy."

"That's a very long name," she said, all sympathetic.

"Yes, yes it is. And you see, that was the problem . . ."

That's how Belinda Mae was born. I'm not sure where the name came from, but suddenly it was there, and I could see the little girl I was inventing. Over the next year, I made up stories for a lot of patients about Belinda Mae's very long name, about her learning to tie her shoes, and about her frenemy, Sophia Tanya.

And one day, I was telling the story to a new patient, when her mother came in. I didn't know then that her mother was the sister of an editor for a children's book publisher. The mother called her sister and told her the story, and then the editor asked the mother to have me call her.

After all the times I'd told those stories, it should have been easy to capture them on paper, but it wasn't. But a couple months later, I sent that editor the first two Belinda Mae stories, and after that . . .

That first editor took me under her wing and taught me a lot about the craft of writing.

*I still volunteer as a nurse at a local clinic when they
need me, but I'm a full-time writer now.*
Thanks to you.
And tonight . . . that will be thanks to you, too.

Love,
Piper

I set the journal aside. I started it the day Ned moved in next door. Was that only a year ago?

Coop was teaching across the street this year. She swore I was going to get sick of her, but I knew I wouldn't. She'd already asked me about helping her with a creative writing class.

The end-of-day bell rang, signaling that the first day of the new school year had officially ended. The front doors of the school burst open and students of every size flew down the steps. Screaming, laughing, running, shouting. As if a day of sitting in their classrooms had taxed them beyond all endurance and that pent-up energy needed some immediate release.

I wondered if that was how it was for Amanda at the end of the school day. Did she walk out of her high school with a group of friends, laughing and talking about their day?

She was a sophomore this year, so the school wouldn't be so strange and foreign . . . unless they'd moved.

Oh, I hope her family didn't move around a lot. I hope she lived in the same house her parents had brought her home to from the hospital and that she had friends from grade school who were still friends in high school.

I could picture a doorway where her mother dutifully marked her height each year on her birthday. And there would be dings and dents throughout the house that would become family stories.

"Do you remember . . . ?" they'd ask each other, and then laugh at the retelling.

I hoped . . .

Those two words pretty much summed it up. I hoped.

I rubbed the soft leather cover of the journal I'd been filling for the last year. It was full of my hopes for Amanda as well as stories.

I didn't write in it daily. No, writing in it was too painful for that. But every few weeks, or sometimes months, I put something down in it. Someday I hoped Amanda would read it and some of these stories would become family stories. "Do you remember . . . ?" she'd ask.

Today, I really didn't have time for writing in it, but still that story about my first sale insisted it go in the book.

To a non-writer a sentence like that would sound insane, but I'd been writing since I was twenty-five. Granted, that was only six years ago. Still, I understood the siren call of a certain story or scene. When that call came, there was no putting it off, or waiting until later. I had a notebook on my nightstand for scenes that came to me in the wee hours. I—

"Hey, Pip," Ned called as he walked across the driveway to my front porch, interrupting my musings.

In the year since he'd moved in, I'd had to admit defeat when it came to getting him to call me by my full first name. I'd been *Pip* to him from the first.

But though I couldn't sway him, the last year had taught me how to tease him appropriately in return.

"Catch any bank robbers?" I asked.

He sighed. "So it's one of those days?" He glanced at the notebook that was still in my hand.

"What do you mean?" I asked.

"Whenever you're working on your laptop, you're all smiles and happiness. Sometimes, I swear butterflies are going to start sliding down rainbows from your keyboard. But on the days you sit here scribbling in that, you're . . . not." Before I could protest, he held up his hand. "Whenever you write in there, it reminds me of a man who's stuck in a bear trap."

That was an analogy I'd never heard before. And frankly, I had no idea how bear traps and journals could connect. "Pardon?"

He looked as if he'd won our sparring match as he explained, "Pulling that trap off hurts, but in the end, he's better for it. Whatever you write in that notebook hurts, but when you're done, you're better . . . until the next time."

I couldn't think of a response to that because the truth of the matter was, he was right.

We'd become friendly, Ned and I. He was the kind of neighbor I could run to for a cup of sugar. If he had it, he'd share with me. But odds are he'd be more apt to run over to my house for sugar, like that first time, or any other pantry item.

That's not to say our neighborliness was one-sided. Ned had been the one who figured out how to open my car door after I accidentally locked my keys in it a few months ago. And when the snow was very heavy and high last winter, he'd sometimes surprise me by snowblowing my sidewalk and driveway, as well as Mrs. W.'s, my elderly neighbor on the other side.

I'd been right that first day . . . he was a good neighbor.

But it was these little front-porch chats—which had morphed into on-the-couch chats when it had become too cold for the porch over winter—that had moved him beyond just a regular wave-at-him neighbor. I might shovel for Mrs. W., but we rarely visited. I'm not even sure if she knew I was a writer. No, it was different with Ned than with the rest of my neighbors.

Soon after the car incident, I'd had a spare set of keys made and kept them at his place, and he gave me his spares, just in case. But we both knew the odds of Ned forgetting his keys or anything else were slim. He was an organized, by-the-book kind of guy.

"Okay, so let's move away from talks of books and bear traps," I said. "You'll be there tonight?"

He nodded. "I will. My boss bought a table for the firm."

Over the last year and our chats, I'd learned that Ned was a retired cop. Not that he was old. He wasn't. But he'd left the police force in Detroit, gotten his private investigator's license here in Pennsylvania, and gone to work for a local Erie law firm. I occasionally teased him by comparing him to *Colombo* or *Magnum, P.I.*, and he habitually tried to convince me his job was nothing like those television detectives. He did all the investigative legwork for the attorneys at the firm. He located and interviewed witnesses and made sure they were at court. He photographed scenes—accident scenes and crime scenes.

He was no Fox Mulder.

We watched a bunch of *X-Files* over the winter, and sometimes I called him Fox. He pretended to find it annoying, but I thought he kind of liked it.

I'm pretty sure that I couldn't do his job, either when he was a cop, or now.

Really, I wouldn't know where to begin.

Maybe that's why I wrote YA books—young adult—rather than hard-core mysteries.

Or romance.

Yeah, romance was definitely not a genre I should pursue.

I laughed at the thought.

"There you go again, Pip." Ned looked amused.

"Sorry. I don't mean to." Things occurred to me at the oddest times—thoughts tumbled over thoughts. Inspiration collided with facts.

"So, what did I say that amused you this time?" Ned asked.

I shook my head. "Nothing. I was just thinking that if I ever decided to change the type of books I write, I probably shouldn't look at romance because, after all, they say writers should write what they know."

His amusement cleared and gave way to his serious look. "There's someone out there for you. Maybe you'll meet him tonight. Mela and I could help you look for him."

Save me from that kind of help from Ned Chesterfield. The only thing worse would be Mela helping. She still didn't like me, but I think she'd finally realized I wasn't a threat to her relationship with Ned.

"Oh, there was someone for me. Once." I shrugged, not wanting to explain that someone was an infant. "You know, the one that got away."

It was very close to a lie. After all, Amanda didn't get away. I gave her away. But puh-TAY-toe, puh-TAH-toe.

"There are other fish in the sea," he said.

I shook my head. "Not for me. I'm a goldfish, happily swimming in my own bowl."

Like my patient who asked me for that first story, I now knew that all good stories started with *once upon a time*. And once upon a time, I'd thought that someday I might marry and have more children, but that was just a story I told myself because the truth of it was, I wouldn't. I mean, what if Amanda came and found me? She'd see the children I kept after giving her away. That was a kind of pain I wouldn't give to anyone, especially not to the child I loved.

Ned smiled indulgently. "Just wait until you meet *him*. That guy who's meant for you. As soon as he comes along, you'll change your tune."

He gave a wave and started toward his house, then turned around. "I'm going to get changed for your shindig. Maybe it's time for you to put away your work and get ready, too?"

"Was that a subtle way of saying my hair needs taming?" I often thought that if my hair was well behaved, being a redhead wouldn't have been too bad, but to have wild hair that had a mind of its own added insult to red-haired injury.

"No," Ned said with a chuckle. "It was a subtle way of reminding you that you can't go to a gala event—especially when you're the host—wearing holey jeans and a T-shirt that says, '*Abernathy's Rules.*'"

I looked down and realized I'd thrown on one of Belinda Mae Abernathy's promotional T-shirts. "You're probably right."

"I always am," he assured me.

I snorted my response. Still, I did get up and head inside. Two hours later, I was primped and polished, as my mother liked to say.

To be honest, my version of *primped and polished* was very different than her version. I knew she'd be at the fund-raiser tonight and she'd be dressed to the nines. I was satisfied with my current six or maybe even seven.

After all, when you lived your life dressed barely above a two, dressing to the sixes or sevens makes for a perfectly acceptable score.

It took me all of ten minutes to drive from my eastside home to Erie's bay. Erie, Pennsylvania is a small, big town. Or a big, small town. I'd used both descriptions in my middle-grade books. And though either way was contradictory, I thought both described Erie to a T. The city on the shore of Lake Erie had somewhere around a hundred thousand residents, but I could drive from my eastside home to the west side of town in fifteen minutes.

So, it only took me and my dressed-to-the-sevens self ten minutes to get to Bayfront Convention Center. And that was with after-work traffic.

Amanda's Pantry's fund-raiser was in the ballroom. The first year, it had been in the convention center's smallest ballroom. This year, the biggest.

I walked in an hour before the big event began. We'd done Amanda's annual fund-raiser here since the first one, and the staff had the setup down to a science.

The large tables were set with ten chairs and place settings. The centerpieces were gorgeous. They were mainly silk forget-me-nots with white roses. The forget-me-not was the flower I'd chosen to use on the Amanda's Closet logo.

I'd always thought that forget-me-nots were not only beautiful, but also resilient. They grew in a well-tended garden as well as in the wild.

My mother and father were the first guests to arrive. They'd supported Amanda's Pantry since its inception. Mom was a school district superintendent and Dad was an English professor at a local college. The doctors George, I jokingly called them. I thought Great-grandmother Rose would have been impressed.

My mother, whose once-red hair had faded to a steely gray, was indeed dressed to impress and pointed at her name tag, which read *Dr. George*. "Really, Piper, Tricia would have been fine."

I laughed. "I say if you've got it, flaunt it." I led them to the head table. "You two are up front."

Mom's table included a few of the principals from her schools. They'd done a district-wide fund-raiser for Amanda's Pantry. We had hundreds of gently worn coats, hats, and gloves to distribute from the food pantry for the coming winter. We called the offshoot Amanda's Closet.

"Thanks, honey," Mom said.

"Thank you. I—"

I didn't have a chance to say more than that because people started to arrive. I positioned myself at the door and greeted everyone. The first year I instituted the name tag rule and in retrospect it was a godsend. Most of the people who came out for our annual dinner were people I saw once a year.

Let's face it; writers who spend most of their time in holey jeans aren't the type to mingle with the city's elite. But my parents ran in educational circles, and slowly local businesses and the political hierarchy had become involved with Amanda's Pantry.

Some of the people were easy to identify and put a name to the face, some not so much. The mayor had been coming to our events since before he was mayor, along with city council members, the chief of police, his deputy chief, and captains. There were representatives from the fire department and water authority, too.

We'd been so lucky that each year there were more and more people who supported us and came out to the event.

This year, Ned's law firm had come as well.

I smiled at the thought, knowing full well that the attorneys Ned worked for certainly didn't think of themselves as working at *Ned Chesterfield's law firm*, but in my mind, the firm was his. It was all about perspective.

I stood next to the door for a half hour, thanking people for coming, pointing to the bar. Helping direct them to the appropriate tables.

Ned came in with Mela on his arm. He looked great in his suit, and Mela looked gorgeous . . . and knew it.

Ned shot me a grin that said he was already teasing me in his mind. "You tamed it."

I shook my head, and I swear that strands of my hair popped out of my bun just to mock me as I said, "I tried."

Ned laughed and kissed my cheek.

Mela smiled at me, but beneath her upturned lips, I saw something else. It was a look that said she was staking her claim. She wanted to be sure I understood Ned was hers. We'd made a truce of sorts. She tolerated my friendship with Ned but sent me little reminders that he was hers.

If she'd asked me, I'd have assured her that I didn't need her reminder.

And beyond that, I might have mentioned that I was pretty sure Ned wouldn't want to have any claim staked on him.

But she didn't ask and I didn't offer.

We had a weird relationship, Mela and I. She was always very nice to my face, but beneath the smiling facade, her dislike was palpable, and I also knew there was nothing I could do to change that.

She simply couldn't or wouldn't believe that I didn't have designs on Ned.

I wasn't sure what I could do to make her feel better about it, other than ignoring him, and I wasn't going to do that. He was a good neighbor. We were friendly, but certainly not best friends. But I'd grown accustomed to, and looked forward to, our talks and our occasional *X-Files* nights. Visiting and teasing Ned had become a welcome part of my daily routine.

He was the kind of neighbor I could call at midnight if I heard something bumping outside . . . or worse, something bumping inside.

Ultimately, I decided that it was Mela's problem, not mine, and simply tried to be nice.

"You look lovely tonight, Mela," I said, meaning it.

Her smile remained in place, as if she'd glued it on and didn't dare let it slip because if she did, her true feelings would explode from her tight grip on them.

"You look . . . uh *good*, too, Piper."

She'd made sure there was the slightest hesitation as she searched for the thesaurus-worthy word *good*. I was sure Ned hadn't noticed it, but I had. I knew that had been Mela's intent.

Mela gave me a regal nod before practically dragging Ned toward the bar.

Ten minutes later, the heads of Ned's firm—Josiah and Muriel Johnson—came in. "Piper, it's so nice to see you again," Muriel said. We'd met at a backyard picnic at Ned's over the summer.

She did a group introduction to some of the other people from the firm. They didn't say if they were other lawyers, aides, or what. I simply smiled and thanked them all for coming and went back to greeting guests.

By the time everyone arrived, I was already exhausted.

I went to a writers' conference once and attended a workshop that talked about extroverts versus introverts. That's when I discovered that I am absolutely an introvert who can put on an extrovert mask long enough for an event like this. But I knew tomorrow, I'd be drained.

As I had that thought, Liz, a reporter from the newspaper, asked if she could talk to me a minute. I pasted a smile on my face, hoping it wasn't as brittle looking as Mela's had been, and that it was extrovertish enough to cover my inner introvert and said, "Of course."

Liz asked about Amanda's Pantry and I recited some of our statistics. And then she asked, "Can you tell me about the Amanda you named it for?"

I nodded. "I'll be covering that in just a minute in my very short speech."

She laughed. "Great. If I have follow-up questions, I'll catch you later?"

"Sure," I told her.

Over the years I'd been asked that same question time after time. Who was Amanda?

No matter how many times I answered it, how many ways I answered it, it was still my most frequently asked question. I knew it was my own fault, but I wouldn't have named the food pantry anything else, because it, along with so many other facets of my life, was for Amanda . . . for her.

Two television news cameras were setting up in the back and the band was set up on the stage. That was good news. Though I hated being on television, I knew that the pantry would probably receive a few more donations because of the coverage.

I was up.

I made my way to the stage, tucked another stray bunch of hair behind my ear, and adjusted the microphone.

"Hello, everyone. I think I greeted all of you as you came into the ballroom, but in case you snuck in through the kitchen," the audience chuckled, "I'll say welcome again. For those who don't know, I'm Piper George. I want to thank you for coming out tonight to support Amanda's Pantry.

"I've been asked countless times, *Who is Amanda?* As a matter of fact, someone asked me again tonight."

I found Liz at the newspaper's table and she smiled and gave me a nod.

"Some have accused me of dodging the question, but that's not it at all. I'm happy to tell you all exactly who Amanda is."

Liz couldn't have known this would be my speech, but her question was perfectly timed. I'd answered this question to individuals since Amanda's Pantry opened four years ago. I'd opened it the same year I'd quit working and started writing full time.

Eventually someone noticed that all my dedications since my very first Belinda Mae book was published were also dedicated to Amanda. So now, I'd tell them.

"Amanda is every child who's going to bed hungry because there's nothing to eat in her house.

"Amanda is every child who is cold because she doesn't have a proper coat to wear in Erie's harsh winters."

She was that little girl at the grocery store back when I was in college. And she was the daughter I'd given up to another family.

I thought those parts, but didn't say them. It's not that my daughter was a secret, but since I'd given her up, I only had my memories of her—my hopes and dreams for her—and my love to hold on to. Those things were too precious to share with anyone else.

So I simply continued my speech, sharing Amanda's Pantry's announcement.

"Giving those children a name seemed to make the issue of hunger more real. I could tell you that according to Feeding America, 15.9 million children in the US live in food-insecure households. They live in homes where going to bed hungry is not only possible, but probable. That number is staggering. And it's easy to believe that one person can't make a difference. So spouting that number, then asking for help seems as if you're asking people to toss pennies into a deep well that has no bottom to it.

"Or, I can tell you that *Amanda* will go to bed hungry tonight without your help. Helping one child seems possible."

After that little girl in the grocery store, I became more aware of people who didn't have enough food, and the thought that it could be Amanda in that situation haunted me. "So Amanda is every one of those 15.9 million children. She is every child who needs a winter coat. And she is every child who faces a difficult time in school because she doesn't know how to read, or doesn't read well.

"The name Amanda means *deserving to be loved*. Every child is that.

"Tonight, I'm happy to announce that Amanda's Pantry and our annual Amanda's Closet will now be offering books, free of charge, to all the Amandas out there."

Every fall, the pantry gave out coats to kids who needed them, but this was a new facet of our services. "And while I'm thrilled with your generous coat and hat donations, and I'm hoping you write a big fat check for the pantry, I am not asking for any donations for the bookshelf. I have corporate donors in some of the country's largest children's books publishers."

I was thrilled about that. Every child who came to the food pantry would receive a book of his or her own. Books—plural—I hoped.

"So, thank you for coming out tonight, and thank you in advance for your generous donations." I leaned close to the mic and in a stage whisper said, "That was a not-so-subtle hint. And now, I'm going to get off the stage and turn it over to the Glenwood Hillbillies. Please, feel free to get up and dance, or just visit with your friends. And please remember to open your hearts and your wallets to *Amanda*."

Mom and Dad were in a deep conversation with the people at their table, so I hurried back to Ned's and collapsed in an empty seat. "Have I ever mentioned that I hate public speaking?" I said to no one in particular.

Ned snorted. "Yes. Every time there's an Amanda fund-raiser."

"Well, at least I'm predictable," I said.

"There has to be more to the name Amanda than you said," Mela sniped.

"Like I said, Amanda means *worthy of being loved*. Every child is that. If I'd called it *The Food Pantry* or *Some Kids' Food Pantry*, it wouldn't have the same sense of immediacy. People who donate to it have a more intimate response when they're giving to a specific name. Amanda was the perfect name for the food pantry."

That wasn't a lie. I'd used the line a hundred times, but this time, it felt like one because Ned was sitting next to me listening and I knew it wasn't the whole story.

It wouldn't have felt as much like a lie if I were just saying the words to Mela.

Ned didn't seem to notice my evasions. He simply asked, "Where's Coop tonight?"

"She had a PTA meeting. Normally, she'd skip, but as a new teacher at the school she felt she had to be there."

He nodded and asked, "Have you met everyone at the table?"

"Mr. Johnson introduced me, but it was a quick-shake-and-nod moment."

He smiled. "That's what I thought." He nodded at the man on the other side of the vacant chair I'd slid into. "So as a reintroduction, this is Anthony Long. The Johnsons brought him on as a partner last month."

Anthony was a nice-looking man who was somewhere between thirty and fifty.

Why is it that men had so many ageless sorts of years? The thing that made me lean more heavily toward the forties than the thirties was the thinning hair on the crown of his head. I respected the fact that he'd shaved it rather than try for a classic comb-over. "Congratulations on making partner, Tony."

"Anthony," he corrected with a smile.

I laughed. "Sorry, Anthony. I know how it feels to have people mess with your name." I looked very pointedly at Ned.

Ned didn't look the least bit abashed. "It's almost as annoying as people who misrepresent your job."

"Those people only pick at your job when you start in on their name, *Fox*."

Mela always looked her most brittle when Ned and I teased each other. Her smile this time didn't reach her eyes. Heck, it hardly reached her lips. "I don't think Ned's job warrants any teasing. That kind of thing is more appropriate for a school-aged relationship than for an adult one."

Normally, I'd just let her social spanking slide, but tonight, I shot back without thinking, "I bet you'd sing a different tune if Ned shortened your name to *Meh*."

This time she didn't even attempt a smile.

Feeling contrite, I tried to move past my less-than-nice comment and asked, "Is Mela short for something?"

She shook her head.

"Do you know what your name means?" I asked.

She didn't shake or nod her head . . . she glared.

I simply waited and finally Mela gave up and said, "Dark."

I thought that was a fairly accurate description of her, but I knew I was being unfair. Mela and I were oil and water. No amount of shaking was ever going to make us like each other. And because Ned liked her, she had to have some good qualities. I just couldn't see them.

Anthony shot Mela a sympathetic look. "I think my mother said *Anthony* meant priceless, or maybe she was just being a mom and saying I was priceless." He chuckled and then asked, "What does *Piper* mean?"

"It's actually a family name. But I guess it's also a name that means what it says. Someone who plays—"

My mother came up behind me. "Piper's about to say her name means someone who plays the flute, and though it's also a family name, her father and I named her Piper because we were on our honeymoon in Scotland when she was conceived and—"

There are certain subjects that are fair conversational topics at a party and some that are not.

The meaning of a name? Fair game. A bit of social conversational frippery.

The place of my conception? Not so much.

I cut my mom off. "TMI, Mom. Really, that's more than anyone here needed to know."

Anthony came to my rescue as he asked, "Would you care to dance?"

I nodded. "I'd love to."

I kissed my mom's cheek as I got up and she whispered, "prude," in my ear.

I whispered back, "Grandma had sex, too."

She laughed and said, "Ew."

Anthony and I were the first ones on the dance floor. "Thanks for saving me. Next thing you know, my mom would have been telling everyone the exact details of that magical night." I made a delicate gagging gesture at the thought.

It made Anthony laugh. "Your mom probably would have gotten along with my mom."

I noticed the past tense and said, "I'm sorry."

He nodded, wordlessly accepting my thanks.

I wanted to change the subject from parental sex and his loss, so I warned him, "I believe in truth in advertising . . . I am not much of a dancer."

"I'm not Fred Astaire, so I don't need a Ginger." He must have realized that the term might not have sat well because of my red hair. "Sorry."

"No problem. Calling my hair ginger is certainly nicer than calling it Medusa, which is my description of choice."

He chuckled again. "Just relax and let me lead."

I did, and Anthony managed to not only lead, but also to make me look almost good in the process. The fact it was *almost* good and not *really* good was on me, not on him.

He talked about relocating to Erie from Pittsburgh. ". . . don't get me wrong; I'm glad I did it. It was a great move for my career. But it's hard to go from somewhere you know to a strange place. Hard to go from a place where you have lifelong friends and family to someplace where you only know your work colleagues."

"I've lived in Erie all my life, but I've always felt a bit like someone on the outside. Not that I don't have friends, but . . ." I shrugged. I did have friends, but I'd never been someone who required a lot of interaction with people. I had my parents, Coop, the people at Amanda's Pantry, the kids at school, and now Ned. That was plenty of people for me.

Maybe when you live with so many characters in your head—and to me, they weren't just fictional characters, but rather people in their own right—there wasn't a need to populate your life with myriad real people.

Really, between all that and my fictional characters, I was good.

Maybe there was a book about a teenager who spent more time with fictional characters than real people. Maybe—

"Piper?"

I realized I'd drifted and poor Anthony was still talking to me. "Sorry. Drifting away is an occupational hazard, at least for me."

"You had an idea for a book?"

I nodded.

"I'd love to hear more about how your process works," he said. "Maybe you'd meet me for dinner sometime?"

"Are you asking me for a date?" I asked, wanting to be sure I had it right. After all, he might simply be someone who was thinking about writing himself and wanted to pick my brain.

He laughed as we twirled around the dance floor. "Is that so hard to believe?"

Rather than admit it was and sound pathetic, I laughed and said, "Of course, I'm going to say *no, your asking was not a surprise at all. I was simply surprised it took you so long to ask.*"

We both continued to laugh as we danced. And though I'd never officially answered his question, we both knew I'd have dinner with him. Before the evening was over, we exchanged phone numbers.

That night Amanda was in the forefront of my thoughts. I pulled off my grown-up clothes and changed into a pair of well-worn yoga pants and a sweatshirt, then took the leather journal and went out to the front porch.

The school had floodlights for security. So at night my front porch was bathed in a soft glow of light that I knew from past experience was just enough to write by.

I loved my porch at night. Some of the neighboring houses had lights shining through their windows. You could tell the ones that came from televisions. They flickered and changed color.

A car drove by. I wondered where they were going so late at night. Were they coming in from some social function, too? Or were they on their way out to meet friends?

At midnight, the neighborhood was very quiet. I could see the school's playground bathed in light, but empty. Silent.

It was as if the hustle and bustle from the day was a distant memory.

I picked up my pen and the noise of the first scratch across the paper seemed amplified in the silence.

Dear Amanda,

When I was pregnant with you, I borrowed a baby-name book from the library. I knew I wouldn't keep you—that I couldn't keep you—though it took me months to admit it. My mother had gone back to school for her doctorate and she offered to quit and help, but that wouldn't have been fair to her or to you. Even with her help, I couldn't have given you the life I dreamed for you. You deserved so much more than a teenage mother who had two years of high school left could give you . . .

As I write those words, I realize you are now the same age I was when I got pregnant with you.

I put down my pen and tried to digest that fact.

I hoped Amanda's mother had talked to her about sex . . . more than that, I hoped Amanda had listened.

I thought about telling her about her father tonight, but I wasn't ready for that yet, not that my story was unique. I thought I knew what love was, but the flash-in-the-pan feeling wasn't love. That sizzle was like a firecracker. It was bright and loud, but burned itself out quickly.

I was so young, not that I realized it at the time. When I was fifteen, I thought I knew it all. I was sure my life would be a fairy tale, and maybe in some ways it has been. I've built a life I love.

But there is a hole in my heart and in my life. That hole is filled with the absence of you. I didn't give you up in order to build a better life for myself, but because I wanted a better life for you.

And though I knew your new parents would give you the name you've grown up with, I needed to name you. I only held you for that hour, trying to store up a lifetime of memories and love in sixty short minutes.

And when the nurse came to take you, she opened the door and I caught the barest glimpse of the parents who would raise you. They looked . . . ordinary for that first second, but as the nurse put you in your new mom's arms, she was transformed. She was absolutely beautiful in her joy. Your dad, too.

As the door swung shut, I called out, "Good-bye, Amanda," and I tried to let you go.

It's been fifteen years and I'm still trying.

Amanda means "deserving of love."

You do deserve that and so much more.

I hope that by giving you to your mother and father, you found love and a happy home.

Love,
Piper

Ned's car pulled into his driveway. Even though I hadn't turned on the porch light, he saw me.

"I just dropped off Mela," he said as he got out of his car. Then he added, "You look more like yourself," as he walked the few steps to the edge of the porch.

I didn't take offense that, in Ned's eyes, looking like myself meant wild hair and oversized sweatshirts. "I feel more like myself. I swear my hair whimpered with gratitude when I took it down."

He laughed, then saw the notebook on my lap. "I'll let you get back to it."

"I was just finishing up and getting ready to head to bed. I don't do late nights very well."

"I've got to go to the office tomorrow, so I need to call it a night, too." But rather than turn to leave, he said, "It was a nice evening. Everyone danced and seemed to enjoy themselves."

"I'm glad. Everyone was very generous."

"Your speech was short, but good. I mean, I know how much you love the limelight."

I snorted my response. "Yes, I do love the limelight. And I'm a huge fan of root canals, too."

For a moment, his teasing ebbed and he looked serious as he said, "I think that makes what you did this evening all the more impressive . . ." he paused and then added, "Pip."

"Thanks, Fox."

"Night," he said, chuckling.

I watched as Ned walked to his own front door. He unlocked it, then gave a little wave before he went inside.

I got up myself and headed inside, the journal clutched in my hand.

Maybe this small, leather-covered book was my bear trap. I'd climbed back into the trap and was now climbing out again.

And I hoped tomorrow, I'd feel better for it.

At least, until the next time.

Chapter Four

As I pulled my car into my driveway that following Sunday, I was reveling in a successful morning of house sales. I couldn't help but think of my mom. She says I am a creature of contradictions. I love fine china, but my idea of fine clothing is a pair of jeans with no holes in the knees.

From the front, my brick house with its big porch and small white dormer jutting out from the roof is as neat and orderly as I can possibly keep it. There are immaculately trimmed hedges along the porch. And *on* the porch, white wicker furniture, a welcome mat, and an antique milk box that my paperboy leaves the paper in.

But my backyard is not neat in the least.

It's overgrown and more than a bit wild looking. In a sea of well-kept lawns, my backyard was the neighborhood anomaly. I'd like to say I felt bad about that, but in truth, my yard is fenced in, so unless my neighbors are standing on something, I don't think it bothers them. At least no one's mentioned it to me if it does.

When I first moved in five years ago, there was a six-foot, solid wooden fence around the yard, but very little grass and no trees or bushes. That first spring, I went to a local nursery and went a bit crazy.

I spent a week planting everything from serviceberry trees to raspberries bushes. Then I added a couple apple trees and a chestnut tree.

That fall, I put in hundreds of bulbs and added more in the spring, then threw three containers of wildflower seeds into any bare bits of earth that were left. Still, I added. Mints, chicory, milkweed, Queen Anne's lace . . .

Sometimes one plant choked out a neighbor, and occasionally something totally unexpected popped up. But five years later, my yard is perfectly imperfect.

It's a chaotic jumble of greenery.

If my front porch was my place to work, then my backyard was my place to dream.

One of the nicest perks about being a professional writer was that daydreaming was part of my job description, and my yard was the perfect place to do that.

I'd gone to a local estate sale. There are a lot in Erie on weekends. One of the guys who worked it helped me load today's prize into my car, but there was no way I was going to pull it out of the car and drag it into the back on my own.

I glanced at the time on my phone. Ten thirty-five. That was a perfectly acceptable time to bother someone. Especially when the someone in question was Ned.

Although, even if I felt it was earlier than was acceptable, I probably still would have bugged him.

I texted him.

Need some help, if you have a minute.

He texted back within seconds.

Where are you?

Out front.

A few minutes later he came out of his house wearing mesh shorts and an FBI Academy T-shirt. He'd gone to the academy when he was still a cop. He'd been at Quantico for four months and from his tales he'd loved every moment of it.

He took one look at my open tailgate and sighed. "What treasure did you unearth now?"

He didn't really need me to answer as he was already in view of my prize.

"Another garden bench, Pip?" He shook his head, clearly not understanding what a true winner I had this time.

"This one's solid iron," I said. "And you can't buy a patina like that."

"Who'd want to?" he groused.

"A lot of people. This bench is practically an antique. And you know what I say—one can never have too many benches." I used my most proper tone.

He snorted as he reached for an end. I got the other end and we carried it alongside the house to the gate. Ned set his side down and opened the gate. "Welcome to Narnia," he muttered.

"Oh, come on," I said as we hefted the heavy bench. "You can come up with a better literary comparison than that."

"Oz?" he tried.

"How about *The Secret Garden*?" I asked. Cooper read that book out loud in school every year. Last year, she'd brought her class to my house to visit afterward.

This year would be easier. She wouldn't need to arrange drivers. The kids could walk across the street, through the gate at the side of my house, and into my yard.

Ned just snorted. "This garden's no secret. The entire neighborhood knows about it. How about the Hanging Gardens of Babylon?"

"Huh?" was my elegant response. Then I chuckled, sure this was another one of Ned's jokes. He was famous for making things up.

"No, really, it's a thing," he said, then asked, "Where's this going?"

"Back by the milkweed." I would never be a master gardener and there were a number of plants in my garden that I couldn't name, but every year I tried to add something and last year, it was milkweed. I hoped I'd have monarchs soon.

"Be more specific," Ned said.

I nodded toward the back corner of my larger-than-average backyard. "The back right-hand side."

"Better. And what you're saying," he started, then dodged a cluster of raspberry bushes, "is you've never heard of the Hanging Gardens?"

Sometimes, it was hard to tell if Ned was teasing. He could do it with an utterly straight face, which probably made him good at his job, but made it impossible to tell if he was being truthful.

"No, I've never heard of them," I said slowly.

He laughed. "It's rare that I know something you don't know."

"Speaking of things I don't know," I said. "Have you noticed how unfair it is that you are willing to call that new attorney at your firm—"

"It's not my firm," he interrupted in order to correct me.

I started again. "You called that new attorney *at the firm you work for* Anthony, not Tony. Why won't you call me Piper?"

We nestled the bench against the fence, right next to the corner of milkweed. After a bit of wiggling it seemed rather level.

I stepped back to look at it and nodded.

I sat down to try it out. My house was virtually hidden by the greenery that separated this seat from it. This would be the perfect place to lose myself in a daydream.

Ned sat next to me and answered my question. "After all that talk about names and their meanings, did you know that *pip* can be short for pipperoo, which can mean *something wonderful*. It's slang, but it's British slang, so I thought you—my proper-teacup friend—would appreciate it."

I gave him a questioning look. Was he teasing about this as well?

He made the childhood symbol for truth by crossing his heart with his index finger. "I looked it up. A couple days after we met. You are most definitely a pip, which is why I call you that."

He said the last bit with a seriousness that made me feel . . . odd. So I snorted, which made him laugh and things were back to normal between us.

And we sat silently in the back of my yard enjoying the view, until Mela called Ned from his back door like some mother calling a child who was late for dinner. "Ned?"

"See you later," he said, already hurrying toward the gate. "You were right to buy the bench," he called over his shoulder. "It fits right there."

Half an hour later, I got a text message from Ned. It was a link to a site devoted to the mysteries of the Hanging Gardens of Babylon.

I laughed.

Dear Amanda,

I'm sitting and writing this on my new bench—well, an old bench I rescued from an estate sale. I rarely write in the garden, but today, I felt compelled.

I'm looking at my milkweed plants. I gave them this entire back corner of my yard. They aren't as pretty as a lot of my flowers, and they aren't edible . . . at least by humans. They actually can burn if you get the sap on you, and if you inadvertently ingest any of the plant, it can make you sick.

So why did I plant them? Because milkweed is the monarch butterfly's only food. I read an article about how necessary it is to the species' survival.

People dug up most patches because they consider it a weed. That's how I thought about them, but this year I had flowers and they were beautiful. Different, but stunning in their own right.

I think it will be fascinating to see the caterpillars munching away on the leaves. Monarch caterpillars eat something that's poisonous, then curl up in a chrysalis and emerge as a butterfly. Frankly, the caterpillars are rather ugly, but they turn into something beautiful. Then they begin the process all over again.

The last generation of butterflies each season migrates to Mexico in the fall. Something that fragile looking can travel such a huge distance.

The butterflies will winter there, then fly back and start the process all over again. I saw a picture of a swarm of butterflies on a tree in Mexico. It was amazing.

Sometimes I think there's a correlation between the monarchs and me. Losing you was bitter, but rather than poison me, it gave me purpose. I started out as a nurse, and I emerged a writer.

But maybe people are like monarchs in more ways than that. Maybe we all repeatedly curl up in a chrysalis and emerge as something else entirely.

I was a child; for that brief hour, I was a mother . . . then a nursing student, then a nurse, then a writer, then a . . .

Maybe we live our lives constantly becoming and rebecoming.

Maybe we're always in the process of metamorphosing into something new.

Love,
Piper

Chapter Five

The Friday after the fund-raiser was one of those perfect autumn afternoons. As summer drifted into memory, the sun hit my porch at a different, lower angle. It came later in the morning and sank under the western horizon earlier.

There was a crispness to the air as a light breeze gusted. It carried the smells of apples and leaves. And though I knew it wasn't so, I would have sworn that I smelled cinnamon.

I had on new jeans that I'd washed three times before putting on this morning. Not a holey knee in sight.

I was trying to work, but it wasn't going well. I had a date with Anthony and though I tried to ignore it, it skittered at the edge of my thoughts all morning.

Thankfully, I had a built-in distraction for the afternoon. I had to go across the street to Cooper's class.

Her eighth graders were writing their own novels. I was Coop's guest *expert* on the matter. I didn't feel like an expert, but she felt I was.

Working with thirteen-year-olds was much different than reading to five- or six-year-olds.

I tried to focus on my work. When I wasn't admiring my holeless knees, I'd been staring at my laptop's screen, waiting for inspiration to strike—it hadn't.

A brown UPS truck slid in front of my house.

I was saved from going through the motions by a delivery.

I closed my laptop and waited with the breathless excitement of a child at Christmas.

I think I love deliveries because there's always a sense of possibility when something arrives. I may be pretty sure it's the box of bookplates I'd ordered, or maybe the new filters for the furnace, but it was just as possible it was something else entirely.

Maybe there was a mysterious letter from an attorney informing me I was the sole heir of a reclusive millionaire. Or maybe I'd won some sweepstakes and they were delivering a prize. Or . . .

I normally knew what a delivery held, but I hadn't ordered anything online lately, so although the UPS man could be bringing me that letter about a massive inheritance, the chances were more likely that he was bringing me something else entirely.

Dave got out of the truck with a large box, which, judging from the way he was carrying it, weighed a lot.

I was pretty sure it wasn't an inheritance, but I was equally sure this was better.

"There's another one in the truck, Piper," Dave said.

"Thanks, Dave," I said.

I was on a first-name basis with my UPS guy, my FedEx guy, and my mailman. I worked alone at home all day. Other than Ned, who worked crazy hours and was sometimes home during the day, my most constant visitors were my delivery people.

Dave went back to the truck and soon plunked a second box down next to the first. "Pretty soon you're going to have to work inside again."

I breathed in deeply. I still thought I caught the faintest scent of cinnamon.

I loved this time of year, but Dave was right, soon enough it would be winter and I'd have to move from my porch to the chair by the window. "You're right. But I've still got a few more porch days."

"I never understood why you write outside so much," he said.

"Okay, this is going to sound totally narcissistic, but I like to work outside in view of the school and anyone who is simply passing by because I feel like if I'm not typing, people are judging me." I laughed. "Yeah, I know, no one is actually noticing me, but still, it keeps my fingers moving across the keyboard." Most days. Obviously not on days I had first dates.

He laughed. "I'll keep that in mind next time I pull up and your fingers aren't flying. I'll judge you." He laughed harder. "Oh, yeah, I'll judge you good. And I'm going to ask my wife to do drive-bys on occasion, and I'll tell her to judge the crap out of you if you're not typing."

"You are a good man, Dave," I assured him.

He was still laughing as he walked back to his truck.

As soon as the brown truck pulled away with a friendly beep goodbye, I opened a box. There it was.

Couch Couch's debut book, *Felicity's Folly*.

I pulled the top book off the pile and admired the cover. Oh, I'd seen it before, but it was always different when the cover was attached to the physical book. I opened it and lost myself for a moment in the smell. It obliterated my fantasy cinnamon and replaced it with the smell of new book.

I wish they could bottle that scent.

As always, I checked the dedication.

And as always it read, *For Amanda*.

I reached back into my ponytail twisty and pulled out a pen I'd shoved there that morning. I scribbled an inscription in the front of the book, then skimmed through it and found the passage on page twenty-seven. I dog-eared that page.

After putting the boxes and my laptop inside the door, I walked across the drive to Ned's front door and knocked.

Mela opened it and in an unguarded moment she glared at me, before she remembered to kill me with kindness and pasted a smile on her face. "What's up, Piper?"

I didn't want to give her the book to give to Ned. I wanted to hand it to him myself. I was saved from having to ask if he could come to the door, which would have annoyed Mela, by Ned himself coming up behind her.

"Hey, Pip, come on in."

I shook my head. "I didn't lock the house up. I just got my author's copies of *Felicity's Folly* and . . ." I thrust the book at him. "Normally my mom claims the first book, but this one's for you. I know that YA is not your normal genre of choice, but . . . well, read the inscription."

I really didn't want to do this in front of Mela, but she stood glued to Ned's side and I'd already started, so I continued. "That first day when you pulled in the drive, I was working on this book. When you came over to the porch, I know I seemed distracted, but it's because when I saw you, I suddenly had a character come to life in my head."

"Yeah, that doesn't sound crazy at all," Mela said in a teasing manner, but I could hear her animosity bubbling among her forced laughter.

I ignored it and continued, "Couch Couch."

"Couch?" he asked.

"Coach Divan. Felicity, the main character, mispronounces *coach* as *couch*. And she knows that a divan is a couch. As I was writing that first scene, you came over and introduced yourself. Ned Chesterfield. I dog-eared the page for you. Did you know that your last name is a name for a—"

"Couch. I did. My father considers it a source of pride and tells people our family invented couches."

I laughed now, just as I had that first day. "Anyway, that's why I laughed when you introduced yourself."

I'd thought about dedicating the book to Ned, but in the end, I couldn't. I wrote the books for Amanda and I couldn't not dedicate them to her. Not even this once. So I settled for adding:

A special thank-you to Ned, who was an inspiration.

I'd written underneath those words:

> *Dear Ned, That day you moved in next door, you not only gave me the gift of inspiration for Couch Couch, you also gave me the gift of your friendship. Thank you for both. Pip*

He opened the book and read the dog-eared page, then looked up at me with a grin. "Yeah, I'm going to work tomorrow and telling everyone that I'm an inspiration."

"Don't let it go to your head. I described you as an everyman sort of guy. I mean, I didn't describe you—Couch Couch—as a male model or anything."

He scoffed. "You've said before that your books are fiction. And they're YA," he added, tossing around the term he'd never heard until he moved in next door to me, "so you couldn't really wax poetic about my rugged good looks."

I snorted. "As if."

"I think you've got rugged good looks," Mela assured him.

Darn. We'd done it again. "I'll let Mela salve your wounded ego," I said, maintaining our banter while distancing myself. "When I get done at the school today, I've got to get ready for my date." I threw that in mainly for Mela's benefit.

She jumped on the tidbit. "You've got a date?"

She didn't have to seem so . . . shocked. "Yes. With Anthony, from Ned's firm. He was at the benefit last week."

Suddenly she seemed friendlier than . . . well, than she ever had. "Oh, he's cute."

"It wasn't so much the cute as the nice that attracted me," I said. "And it's just dinner."

"That was our first date, too. Remember, Ned? He took me out on his friend's boat and we had a picnic—"

Ned cut her off. "Anthony's a nice guy."

"Well, you did say you'd introduce me to someone."

"I did." And though he smiled, I could sense that something was wrong.

I figured that he'd finally noticed Mela's barely hidden animosity. And because I didn't want to be the cause of any friction between them, I said, "That first dinner for the two of you sounds lovely. Anthony and I are going to Alto Cucina."

"Oh, that's nice," Mela said and for the first time ever sounded almost friendly as she added, "Let me know how it goes."

Maybe if I dated someone, she'd finally accept that Ned and I were just neighbors. Well, friendly neighbors.

I nodded. "I will. But before tonight's date, I have a date with a roomful of eighth graders. My cup runneth over."

Ned lifted the book. "Thanks again, Pip."

"You're welcome." I added a, "Bye, Mela," and beat a hasty retreat.

I called Mom to tell her that my copies of *Felicity's Folly* were in. She wanted to come right over, but I explained I'd be out. I offered to leave her book in the door, but she decided to wait until after school. She knew about the date and probably wanted to help me get ready, hoping she could bump me from dressed to the sevens-ish to dressed to the nines. I hated to disappoint her, but I was pretty sure seven was as far as I could go.

At one, I headed over to Coop's class.

Coop had thirty-two eighth graders this year. She'd taught all over the school district, and I was thrilled that this year she'd landed across the street from me. It was nice to have her stop by for a quick chat occasionally after school.

I'd been the story time lady for the younger grades for years. Generally kindergarten, but sometimes through second grade. I read stories, sang songs, and basically had a wonderful time with them. My singing voice is less than stage quality, but the wonderful thing about young kids is, they don't care. Rumor has it, I sing a mean rendition of *"I Have a Rooster,"* and don't even get me started on my expertise with *"Up on the Housetop"* at Christmas.

I would not sing around the older students because I was pretty sure they wouldn't be as forgiving as the kindergarteners.

The office staff buzzed me in. I signed the required sheet and Mrs. Rose asked how the new book was coming. I'd given her my reason for working on the front porch a couple years ago, and ever since she always asked about my current book, as if to prove to me she was checking, though we both knew she couldn't technically see my porch from her seat behind the counter. And since I'd never arrived and not seen her behind the counter, I doubted she was actually checking on my writing often.

"The new book came," I said, holding it aloft. "I brought it to show the kids in Coop's room."

"They'll be excited. And I'll be adding it to my Christmas gift list. You'll be signing it at the convention center for the expo?"

Once a year there's a big expo for women at the convention center on the bay. All kinds of women-centric businesses come out, and one of the local bookstores has a table there and asks me to come sign.

I rarely did book signings, but this annual event was a great way to get out and meet local readers. The expo had added a Teen Scene Night last year. It had been a big hit with local girls, and I'd had a Question-and-Answer hour that had been fun.

"I'll be there," I promised.

"Good. I get most of my Christmas shopping for the grands done by stopping at your table."

"Thanks, Mrs. Rose."

I was unbelievably lucky to have garnered so much support in the community. It wasn't just the expo and other events I was invited to. It was people like Mrs. Rose, who bought my books for their grandkids. And it was the kids themselves who bought my books.

I walked up one flight of stairs to the second floor and looked at the posters as I went. There was a school play for Thanksgiving. I knew I'd probably go because I knew so many of the kids.

There would be a science fair in November as well.

I remembered my award-winning science fair project. I'd studied the effects of sound on plant growth. The plant I talked to and played classical music for grew better than the plants I never talked to or played any music for.

Thinking about Bach, I entered Coop's class.

And I felt a moment's yearning for some soothing classical music.

There was nothing soothing about Cooper's classroom.

"Just back from lunch," she practically shouted as I came in.

When I graduated high school, I thought about being a teacher. The noise level in Cooper's class made me decide that nursing had been a much better option, and writing even better yet.

"Okay, class, find your seats," she shouted.

And while there was still an undercurrent of noise, it was in the tolerable range. "Ms. Pip is volunteering her time, so the least you all can do is pay attention. She's not used to this kind of hullaballoo."

The classroom settled. Although I would have sworn that there was still an undercurrent of sound floating just under the surface of their quiet. As if with the slightest provocation, the noise level would rise again.

"Miss Cooper's right; writing is a quiet business," I explained. "Most of the time, the only sound I hear comes from my fingers tapping on the keyboard and an occasional car driving by my house."

The class finally settled. There was a different feel to the room. I leaned against Coop's desk and started. "Now today, Ms. Cooper said she wanted us to start by discussing creating fictional characters. I thought I'd tell you how it works for me. And for me, it's never the same way twice. Sometimes I have to work really hard to find my character, and sometimes . . ."

I launched into the story of meeting Ned and Couch Couch. The kids listened and then spent a half hour asking questions before Coop put them to work on their own characters.

"Introduce your characters to me," she instructed her students. "How are they the same as you? And how are they different?" Like magic, the room was silent as they went to work.

She motioned me to the hall. "I'll be watching through the window, so no shenanigans," she warned.

"Did you ever listen to warnings like that from your teachers?" I asked. To the best of my knowledge, listening to rules had never been Coop's strong suit, but then again, maybe she'd been better behaved before I met her in college.

She snorted at the thought. "No. But let's not tell them that." She added, "Sorry I missed the fund-raiser last week."

"How'd the PTA meeting go?"

"It wasn't too bad. I met a number of my kids' parents. I think this year's class is going to be a good one. They're excited about the books. Thanks again for the help. I know you're more at home with the little kids."

"I think I'm going to enjoy the older students." To be honest, the kids were so much closer to Amanda's age. I'd spent the class wondering what type of student she was. Would she be like Kelsey and ask question after question because she wanted to be sure she understood the topic completely? Or would she be like the boy in the back row who'd zoned out the entire talk?

Was Amanda a quick study, or did it take her some time to catch on to a new subject?

Was she creative?

Was she—?

"Do you want to do something tonight?" Coop asked, interrupting my stream of thought.

"I'd love to," I said, meaning it, "but I've got a date."

Coop couldn't quite cover her look of surprise.

"Really, Coop, I do date." Then for the sake of honesty, I added, "On occasion."

She was a good enough friend not to point out that it had been a while since my most recent occasion. "So who is he, what does he do, what does he look like? . . . Spill."

"His name's Anthony, he's a partner at Ned's firm—"

"I'm sure the partners enjoy hearing the firm referred to as Ned's."

I chuckled because I'd had the same thought before. I finished, "—and he's good-looking without being intimidatingly good-looking, if you know what I mean."

"Tony sounds nice. Anything else?"

"Anthony. Not Tony," I corrected. "I don't know much else other than he can dance and he has a sense of humor. Plus, in addition to the firm's donation, he made a nice personal donation to the pantry."

"He had you at *donation*," Coop teased. "Speaking of which, do you want a hand tomorrow?"

The first and third Saturday of every month were my days at the pantry and Coop frequently came to help. I nodded. "I'd love it."

"Great. Of course, this time I have an ulterior motive. Between clients, you can tell me all about the date."

"I don't know how much there will be to tell. We're just two people getting to know each other." He seemed nice enough, but I'm not sure that "nice enough" was enough, although I wasn't sure Coop would allow for the distinction.

"Maybe there will be more to tell than you think." She wiggled her eyebrows and grinned.

I doubted there would be anything eyebrow-wiggling worthy about the date but promised to share the highlights with her. I said good-bye and headed home.

Mom was waiting for me on the porch. "Your father had to run some errands so he dropped me off so I could pick up my book and help you get ready for your date," she announced.

I was right, she wanted to dress me to the nines, but a couple hours later, even she had to admit that seven was about as high as it was going to go.

"Seriously, I don't know where you got this hair," she muttered as she tried to capture another escapee.

"Dad always maintained the postman," I teased.

"He'll be here soon," she said.

"The postman?" I asked, trying to look serious.

She shook her head. "I might not know where you got the hair, but that weird sense of humor is all your father's."

"Well, don't forget your book." I padded over in bare feet because I refused to put my heels on one moment sooner than I had to.

She checked the inscription, which read, "To Mom, As Always. Love, Piper."

"To Amanda," she said, reading the dedication. She looked up. "Honey, after all these years, don't you think it's time to let go?"

"I—" I was interrupted by my father beeping the horn.

We both knew it was him because no one else beeped to the rhythm of *"Shave and a Haircut."* He knocked on doors to the same beat. It was nice you always knew it was my dad before you opened the door.

And thanks to him, I was saved from once again trying to convince my mother I was not brokenhearted.

"Go out and show your dad how nice you look," Mom commanded, carrying her book and heading out.

I put on my heels and followed her. It was a bit breezy out and I swear, I could feel my curls blowing loose as I walked.

"You look nice," Dad said on cue without getting out of the car.

"Thanks. Mom was hoping for better than nice, but I'm satisfied with just nice," I teased, trying to push a stray piece of hair behind my ear.

"You look lovely and that is indeed better than nice," Mom retorted. "Tell her, JP."

"Lovely for sure," he agreed.

"Thanks." They pulled away and I resisted a sigh of relief. I adore my parents, but my mother worried far too much about me. I was thirty-one and had proven quite capable of taking care of myself.

I went back into the house and realized the door had blown shut. And my door automatically locked when it was closed.

I didn't even have a cell phone.

I might have worried, but Ned's car was in the drive. I knocked on his door, praying Ned, not Mela, opened it.

He did.

"Can I have the key to my house, please?" I asked.

"Wow," he said as he looked at me.

I pushed my dress down, and then dragged a stray curl from my cheek to behind my ear. "Thanks, I think."

"You're welcome. You do look nice," Ned said.

There it was . . . *nice* again. Mom would not be pleased.

"Locked yourself out again?" he asked.

"No place to tuck keys in a getup like this."

"Come on in before you go all Marilyn in that wind."

It took me a minute to realize that he was referring to Marilyn Monroe. I stepped into his house as he walked down the hall to the kitchen. To be honest, Ned came to my house far more often than I came here. I'm not sure why. His house was a nice enough place. And he wasn't one of those single guys who live in a mess just because they could.

No, his place was probably far neater than mine, but that was because Ned's place was Spartan.

Ned had the bare minimum of furniture. A couch, a recliner, and a huge flat-screen television that dominated the living room.

I'd never been up to his bedroom, but I imagined it was much the same. A bed. A dresser. And not much else.

He came back with the key. "You could have come in."

"I wanted to keep an eye out in case Anthony showed up early."

"He's not an early kind of guy," Ned said. "Or a running-late kind of guy. He's the kind of guy who shows up precisely on time. Someone solid you can count on."

He didn't sound convinced that those were good traits, but I thought they were. "Good to know."

"Have a nice time," he said.

"I will. Thanks."

Rather than going back inside, he followed me across the driveway to my porch. "I'll take the key back because odds are you'll need it sooner rather than later."

"I've only locked myself out a couple times."

He snorted. "I've only had the key a year and this is your third time. So that means you lock yourself out an average of once every four months."

"You locked yourself out once as well."

"No. Mela did. She left to go home while I was out on a walk and locked the door, not realizing I didn't have a key. So technically, she locked me out."

I used the key and handed it back to him just as a car pulled in the drive. "And that's my cue," Ned said. "Have a good time."

Ned stopped to shake Anthony's hand as my date got out of his car. Then Ned went inside and left just Anthony and me. I held the door open as I waited for Anthony. I swear I could feel my curls bopping their way out of my mother's styling.

"Hi," I said as he came up on the porch. "I just have to run in and grab a coat and my purse."

"No hurry. We've got time."

I wasn't sure what to do, so I said, "Do you want to come in?"

"Sure." He stepped inside and I knew the hall he was looking at was the antithesis of Ned's. He glommed in on my antique, cast-iron firefighter symbols. "I like these."

"They were my grandfather's. My mother's father. He was a fireman here in town. Dad's dad was a teacher." I'm not sure why I added that. It didn't have anything to do with the firefighter symbols and it felt awkward.

"My grandfathers were both railroad men," Anthony said. I think he said it more to put me at ease than from any dire need to share his grandfathers' occupations.

I grabbed my coat and purse, checking that I'd put the house keys in my bag. "Shall we?" I said, praying the rest of the evening would be less . . . well, stilted.

Three hours later, when Anthony brought me home, I knew that my prayers had not been answered.

Chapter Six

. . . that first date with Anthony was an awkward one at best. His idea of reading for fun was picking up some dusty historical tome. I read fiction.

Anthony was from Pittsburgh and found Erie's very small-townish qualities almost claustrophobic sometimes, he said.

I complained that it was a long drive from my east-side home to the west side of town.

It took twenty minutes on a bad traffic day.

Anthony loved sports.

I loved Broadway.

I came home sure that I'd never hear from him again.

He called the next day while I was working at the pantry with Coop.

I came home and listened to the message.

He wanted to go out again next Friday.

I guess what I'm saying is, sometimes opposites do

*attract, Amanda. And sometimes, just because something
is difficult, it doesn't mean it's not worth trying.*
    Sorry. I didn't mean to write a lecture.

    Love,
    Piper

⚓ ⚓ ⚓

Two weeks after Thanksgiving, Ned was on my front porch with a Christmas tree in hand.

"Surprise," he hollered and leaned it up against the railing.

We hadn't seen much of each other since before Thanksgiving. He'd gone to New York with Mela to spend the holiday with her family. I'd gone to my parents and I'd taken Anthony. Not out of some passionate need to share a holiday with him, but because he was alone in a new city and wasn't going home to Pittsburgh for the holiday.

No one should spend a holiday alone.

I made sure that Mom and Dad understood Anthony wasn't *the one*. He was a nice guy and we were dating, but I'm pretty sure he didn't feel I was "the one" either.

I don't write romance, but I do believe that there's someone for everyone, and I was pretty sure that Anthony wasn't my someone, but he was a nice guy and we'd gone out a few times since that first date.

"Thanks, Ned," I said, looking at the tree.

"I thought I'd help you set it up," he said. "Mela's out of town on business."

"Sorry," I told Ned. "You know I'd love to, but Anthony got us tickets to *La Bohème* up at Mercyhurst. Why don't you leave it on the porch and we'll set it up tomorrow?" I motioned him inside. "It's freezing out there. I think the weather guys got it right and we're going to have snow tonight."

Rather than remark on the weather, Ned said, "You hate opera."

"Don't you dare tell Anthony that. He knows I like Broadway and thought I'd enjoy it. And I might like opera. I try to be open-minded."

Anthony had been so pleased that he'd gotten us tickets. I got the impression that he thought if it was on stage and had music, it must be something I'd like. I didn't have the heart to tell him that there was a big difference between Broadway and opera. And I had only ever seen one opera. Maybe I did like it and just didn't know it.

"Oh, come on," Ned scoffed. "Open-minded you're not. You're the one who refuses to try sushi because you're sure you won't like it."

"There is a difference between raw fish and opera." I didn't add that I wasn't sure there was *much* of a difference.

"Yeah, sushi's good and opera is . . ." Ned paused dramatically, then added, "well, opera is opera."

"So says the more close-minded of the two of us." Just to tease, I added, "I bet Anthony could get two more tickets and you and Mela could join us."

Ned scoffed. "She's out of town, remember? But you and I both know you're not going to like it."

"We'll see."

⚜ ⚜ ⚜

When Anthony dropped me off, I knew that Ned had been absolutely right—I did not like opera.

It turned out, neither did Anthony.

Oh, he tried to make out like he'd enjoyed himself, but we both knew that was a lie . . . one that we could laugh over.

When he pulled up to my house later, he said, "Maybe I could come in tonight?"

I liked Anthony. He was a pleasant companion, but there was no *spark* between us. I wasn't sure what else to call it, but I knew it existed.

I'd felt that spark with Amanda's father when I was fifteen. I think I'd been looking to recreate it ever since.

But maybe that wasn't as important as I'd thought. Maybe it was just a spark of childish first love, and an adult sort of love was built on more than that flash of fire.

Maybe something that burned cooler but steady was better.

I looked at Anthony and I nodded. "I think I'd like that."

Anthony smiled. "So would I."

⚕ ⚕ ⚕

After that night, we had that added element to our dating. But I wasn't sure it drew us closer like I'd hoped.

But we were becoming linked in other people's minds. Even my parents.

Anthony and I spent Christmas together. He came to my parents' house Christmas morning and stayed for dinner. My mother was impressed that he pitched in and helped with the cleanup. And he'd brought presents for everyone. A nice bottle of whiskey for my father. A beautiful silk scarf for my mother.

And for me? He'd found an autographed copy of Heinlein's *Have Space Suit—Will Travel*.

"Oh, Ned—" my mother said, then quickly corrected herself. "*Anthony*, Piper loved Heinlein as a kid."

"I know," he said. "I went browsing through her bookshelf and found her collection of Heinlein books. Her copy of the *Space Suit* was the most decrepit looking of the bunch, so I figured it was a safe bet."

I hugged him and was so thankful I'd come up with something brilliant for him. "Here."

I handed him the thin envelope. He pulled out two tickets to a Pittsburgh Penguins hockey game.

Ned had suggested them, and from the look on Anthony's face, it had been a great idea. "I talked to a lady at the box office and she assured me these were great seats and you'd be happy. I thought you could ask one of your buddies to go with you," I added quickly, just in case he felt he had to invite me out of politeness.

I did not want to go all the way to Pittsburgh to watch a hockey game . . . match? Didn't matter what you called it; I didn't want to go.

"You're sure you don't want to go with me?" he asked.

My parents said, "She's positive," in unison as I said, "Absolutely sure."

We all laughed.

It was a nice Christmas.

I still didn't feel a huge spark for Anthony, but whatever there was deepened into a warm glow.

Maybe that was better than a spark. Maybe it would be easier to maintain.

When Anthony brought me home Christmas night, he seemed to be waiting to be invited in, but despite the nice Christmas, I didn't want company.

So I kissed him after mentioning how tired I was, then I said good night and thank you for a lovely day.

When I got inside, I sat in front of the tree Ned had brought me and took the small box from under it.

Inside there was a small gold charm. This year, it was a car. Amanda had turned sixteen in August and I knew there was a good chance she was driving by now. And if she wasn't driving, she almost certainly was thinking about it.

I'd brought down the journal earlier and I reached for it now. I noticed how worn the soft leather was becoming. I'd filled almost half of the pages.

As I sat under the rainbow-colored lights from the tree, I knew that when I finished with this notebook, I'd put it in the chest with all the letters from Amanda's Pantry, and all the little gifts I'd bought her over the years.

This charm would join the rest.

Dear Amanda,
Merry Christmas. It's evening now and you were on my mind all day.

I bought you a car charm this year. I wonder if you're driving.

If you are, be careful. I worry.
I'm sure your mom and dad do, too.

I spent the day with my parents and a man I care about. At first, I worried that I didn't feel the same passion for him that I felt for your father, but I've realized that I'm no longer a child and maybe a quiet caring is better.

You're sixteen now. I was sixteen when you were born.

And that's why tonight seems like the perfect night to tell you about your father.

I was a geek in school. I was that girl who always had her nose in a book—books that weren't part of any class assignment. I'm sure you know the type, and maybe if it's genetic, you are the same type yourself.

Over the years, my classmates had grown accustomed to my oddities and they seemed content to just let me be.

I was a sophomore when your dad moved to our school. Mick. His last name was Grant. George and Grant. We frequently sat next to each other in classes that assigned seats alphabetically. His locker was right next to mine as well.

Mick was not a geek.

He was a basketball player, but, oddly enough, he didn't seem to notice any of the cheerleaders who tried to catch his eye. He noticed me.

By that Halloween, we were an item.

By Thanksgiving, we were intimate.

I took a pregnancy test when I missed my period.

I was so scared telling him the news.

I think I avoided telling you this story because I don't want to paint him in a bad light. So, let me be sure to remind you that he was young and his reaction . . . well, I'm sure it would have been different if he'd been older.

He denied he was your father . . .

I stopped writing.

After his denial, Mick had suggested an abortion and said he'd drive me and pay.

I declined.

There was no need to tell Amanda that part.

I wouldn't lie to her in this book, but that wasn't anything she needed to know.

I declined to have an abortion, then went home and truly thought about what to do. I wanted this baby. I'd thought that somehow Mick and I would make it work, despite how young we were. In my fantasy, I thought that we'd marry and raise our child together. I was sure my parents would help us.

But when Mick denied he was the father and suggested the abortion, that childish fantasy shattered. For a day, I thought I might keep the baby and raise it on my own, but in the end, I put aside my childhood and became an adult. I tried to decide what was best for my baby. During the rest of the pregnancy, I tried to find a way out of giving the baby up for adoption, but each scenario only served to convince me I had to do what was right for her. A sixteen-year-old mother was not it.

Two weeks later, I told my parents. They were marvelous. I asked if I could go away for the rest of my pregnancy. And I told them I'd decided to give you up for adoption.

They stood behind both my decisions.

I told them I wanted to go to Ohio and stay with Aunt Bonnie. My mother, your grandmother, was working toward her Ph.D. in addition to teaching. I didn't want the stigma of having a pregnant teen daughter to follow her.

I was so relieved when Mom and Dad agreed that I could go to Ohio. Aunt Bonnie agreed, which we all knew she would. And we told the school that I was finishing out the school year in Europe.

My aunt helped me screen potential parents for you. We both fell in love with your parents. In the trunk, I've put the letter they wrote to potential birth mothers.

I haven't read it in years, but they described themselves as normal and average. Your father was a professor and your mother was an elementary school teacher. They sounded like my parents, and I knew I couldn't give you a greater gift than parents who were as wonderful as mine.

I caught only a glimpse of them as they picked you up. They looked normal. Bland, even.

Until the nurse handed you to your mom.

At that moment, they were transformed. Your mom was so beautiful. They were head over heels in love with you. And in that split second, I knew they were meant to be your parents.

And so I let you go.

But that briefest of glimpses has been something I've held onto all these years.

I hope they were—are—as marvelous as my parents are.

The last time I saw Mick was to have him sign the adoption papers. The caseworkers told me that the adoption couldn't go through without his signature.

We met at a restaurant outside of town a month before you were born.

He didn't ask any questions about me or about you. He simply took the papers, signed them, and got up and left.

When I returned to school for my junior year of high school, he wasn't there. I heard he went to the local Catholic all-boys high school. Their sports programs were always on the news and occasionally, they'd mention his name.

Later, I heard he was going to Notre Dame, and though he didn't make the team, he planned to walk on and try out.

I never heard if he made it.

I haven't heard of him since those high school newscasts, and I haven't spoken to him since he signed the adoption papers.

If I could, I'd have avoided telling you about Mick. I'd like to think he's grown up and would welcome you with open arms if you ever look for him. But I wanted you to be prepared if that wasn't his reaction. If you ever want to find him, you have his name and a few facts, so that should give you enough to point you in the right direction.

I hope finding out about him didn't hurt too much.
I'll confess, I didn't tell you about him sooner because I
was afraid telling you about him would hurt you and
hurt me. But I'm fine. I so hope you are, too.

The clock chimed in the hallway.

It's midnight, Amanda. Another Christmas is over.
I hope it was a wonderful one for you.
I hope it was filled with love, laughter, and family.
Know you've been in my thoughts all day.
You're in my thoughts every day.

Love,
Piper

Chapter Seven

I love April. The world comes back to life. More specifically, my backyard comes back to life with its dizzying array of blossoms and buds.

I added pawpaw trees to a blankish space along Ned's side of the yard. I'd never had a pawpaw and knew it would be a few years before they produced fruit, but I was willing to wait.

I loved the sense of new beginnings that permeated everything in the spring.

I also loved that some of the year's anticipated blockbusters came out. This year, the newest installation of the *Star Trek* reboot was hitting the theaters. I couldn't wait. My inner geek flag was flying as I tried to contain my excitement.

If Anthony was not a fan of Broadway shows or opera, he was even less excited by science fiction.

As someone who grew up reading Heinlein's young adult fiction, the genre was my particular delight. And a few months after Ned moved in, I learned it was his, too. Since Cooper and Mela both disliked the genre almost as much as Anthony, Ned and I went to the midnight opening.

It was almost three in the morning when Ned pulled into his driveway and we were still in the thick of our movie critique. ". . . and I love how Abram's . . ." My comment faded when I noticed Mela's car was parked on the street in front of Ned's house.

At that moment, Ned's front door opened and Mela stepped out onto his porch. She did not look happy.

Not happy at all.

"I'll see you tomorrow," I said and hightailed it into my house.

Yes, I'll admit, it was cowardly, but sometimes the greater part of valor was knowing when to retreat.

I'd planned to go straight to bed to gear up for the next day. This was my Saturday for Amanda's Pantry and I'd promised to go in and help at the health clinic Friday afternoon. Since it was after midnight, Friday was today.

Man, I needed to get some sleep.

But I couldn't manage it.

I'd doze off, then I'd wake up with a start and worry about Ned.

I gave up on the idea of sleep at five. While the water in my tea-kettle heated, I checked and Mela's car was still out front.

Still in my pajamas, which were a pair of old yoga pants and a tank top, I put on an oversize sweater and I took my favorite forget-me-not teacup into the backyard. I sat on the bench in the back corner of the yard and, though I tried not to, I worried some more about Ned.

Mela didn't like that Ned and I had been friendly neighbors since the day he moved in, and over time, we'd become more than simply friendly . . . we were friends.

I'd hoped that the fact I was with Anthony—that Ned had introduced me to Anthony, for Pete's sake—would assuage Mela's concerns, but if her expression last night was any indication, it hadn't.

Normally, I found peace in my backyard, but just as I'd found no sleep last night, I found no peace this morning.

My tea grew cold in my cup. I was just thinking about making another one when the gate on Ned's side of my fence flew open.

For a moment, I thought it was him, coming to tell me not to worry, that everything was okay between him and Mela.

But it wasn't Ned. It was her.

"Hi, Mela," I said, trying to pretend I didn't notice that she was glaring at me.

She ignored my attempt at pleasantries and simply said, "I came to tell you that you won."

"Won?" I asked, sounding as genuinely confused as I was.

She stood in front of me, hands planted on her hips, and glared. "I've broken up with Ned."

"How does that make me a winner? I never wanted—"

She interrupted me. "I can't compete with you. *Saint Pip* who writes stories for kids. Saint Pip who donates her time to feeding the hungry and nursing the sick. Saint freaking Pip. Well, you've won."

"I'm no saint, Mela," I said softly. "And I have never been your competition."

She stared at me for a moment that felt like a slice of forever, then slowly she said, "You really believe that, don't you? You really believe that you and Ned are just friends."

"Of course I do, and of course we are. I'm dating Anthony. Ned and I are neighbors and friends. Just friends."

Mela snorted. "I think it makes it worse that you don't know." She paused a moment, as if weighing the notion, then nodded. "Yes, yes, it makes it worse."

She didn't say anything more, just turned around and walked toward her car. Her shoulders were slumped in defeat and I felt like I should apologize to her.

I heard her car start and after a moment, I couldn't hear it anymore. She was gone and I was torn. I wasn't sure if I should go over to Ned's or simply leave him alone.

I decided to give him some space.

Still, Mela's words haunted me. I tried to take a true measure of my feelings for Ned. I'll admit, the day he'd moved in, I had felt a bit of a . . . no, I wouldn't say spark, but I did notice him. Maybe it would have developed into something more than noticing, but I'd found out he was seeing Mela and that was that. Now, I did feel a warm rush of friendship whenever I thought about him. And that was better than some fly-by-night spark that faded almost as soon as it started, as far as I was concerned.

Lovers came and went, but friends would always be there.

At that thought, I knew I couldn't wait for Ned to come to me. A friend didn't wait to be needed.

I knocked on his door.

I didn't hear anything inside and was about to go back home and call and leave a message, when the door finally opened.

Neither of us bantered or teased, or even smiled. I just asked, "Are you okay?"

He hesitated a moment, then nodded. "I will be. How did you know?"

"Mela came over to tell me that I won. That she'd finally broken up with you because of me. Ned, I need you to know, I value your friendship, but I never would have wanted to come between you and Mela."

"You didn't," he assured me. "And that's not how it went. She didn't break up with me; I broke up with her."

With some men, I might have questioned whether or not they were being totally accurate about who did the breaking, but I knew Ned wasn't like that. I'd never seen him pretend to be anything other than what he was . . . a very nice guy. "Why did you break up with her?"

"It's been coming for a long time," he admitted. "When I was out of town on that case last week, I realized that I didn't miss her. There was no sense of anticipation when we talked at night, no longing for her. And I thought of your parents."

"My parents?"

He nodded. "When I see them together, I can't imagine one without the other. You said when your dad went to that conference a few months ago your mom was over every night because she couldn't stand the empty house."

When Dad had left, Mom said she was excited to spend time with me. She was over every night. She "helped" me clean out my closet, then took me shopping for new clothes to replenish it. We went out to eat and saw two movies. We talked and laughed a lot. I really think she enjoyed the extra time with me, but I also think my mom wasn't sure how to be her without my dad around. "You're right; I think all our girl time was more about her missing him."

"They reminded me of my parents," he said.

His parents lived in Seattle. They were getting on in years and didn't travel much, but he visited them as often as he could.

"My parents are like that . . . incomplete without the other. And my bosses," he continued. "Josiah and Muriel are like that, too. Your parents are quiet and strike me as people who rarely fight, but you know Josiah and Muriel always fight. They fight about cases, about the firm. I think they're both attorneys because they like to fight. That comes through in their relationship. But even with that, I can't imagine them apart."

I'd met Josiah and Muriel more than once, but had only heard about their legendary arguments secondhand from Ned and Anthony. But Ned was right, they fit . . . they functioned as two parts of a whole.

Quietly he admitted, "I realized that I *could* imagine myself apart from Mela. And I finally admitted that wasn't fair to her, or to me."

"Still, if I had anything to do with it—"

He cut me off. "You didn't. The fact that she distrusted you so much only illustrates my point. If we were truly meant to be together, she'd have known that I could never, would never, cheat."

Even though he was saying it wasn't me, I still felt guilty. "Can I do anything?"

He started to shake his head, but then nodded. "Yes. Let's go sit in your backyard and watch the stars give way to the sunrise."

"It'll be freezing," I warned him.

"When has that ever stopped you?"

I smiled at him. "Never. Come on then." I took his hand in mine and gave it a squeeze. "You'll find someone else someday."

He didn't say anything; he just squeezed my hand back.

And we went and sat on the bench in my jungle-ish backyard and watched the stars in silence for a very long time. Slowly, they all gave way to the orange-pink sunrise.

And it wasn't until he spoke a long time later that I realized we still held hands. "Thank you," he said.

"That's what friends are for," I assured him.

And I realized that's what we were. Friends.

Not just neighbors. Not just friendly neighbors. Not even just friends.

He was the type of friend that, if I called and needed him, would drop everything to help me.

We were the type of friends that if one of us moved from here, we'd still be connected. Our friendship began because of proximity, but it had grown beyond that.

I would have sat on that cold bench, not saying anything, and held his hand all day if he needed me to.

That's the kind of friends we were.

> *Dear Amanda,*
>
> *Ned broke up with his girlfriend. I realized he was the type of friend I could call in the middle of the night to come bail me out of jail. Or jump my car. Or . . . The point is, I could call him whenever and for whatever I needed.*
>
> *It made me think of Aunt Bonnie. I know I mentioned her to you before. She's the one I stayed with through the last few months of my pregnancy.*
>
> *When I told my parents I'd decided to give you up for adoption, my mother started to cry and my father said,*

"Piper, I wish we could make this decision for you. It's probably the most difficult decision you're ever going to have to make. You're turning sixteen in a week—that's so young to be carrying a burden like this. But there's nothing to do for it. This has to be your decision, and your mother and I will support you no matter what you decide."

"I'm going to go stay with Aunt Bonnie and find this baby's real parents. I know it's not me, so they have to be out there somewhere, waiting for me to find them and let them know I have their child."

My mother was still crying, but my father nodded. "I'm sure Bonnie will help."

He was right, of course, because Bonnie Masters was his friend, in the same way Ned was mine.

Dad and Aunt Bonnie had grown up next door to each other. They'd gone to school together, even college together. Aunt Bonnie was my godmother. And she became one of my mother's best friends, too.

She was family.

Not one of us doubted that she'd say yes and welcome me with open arms.

Which is exactly what she did.

As I sat with Ned, I realized he was my Aunt Bonnie. He was more than a friend . . . he was family.

I hope your life is full of friends like that.

Love,
Piper

Chapter Eight

In June, I was offered a contract for a short story that would be part of an anthology my publisher was putting together for the following summer. I was thrilled that they'd asked me to be a part of *Summer Nights*. So many authors I loved and admired were contributing.

The day my editor called, I started work on my story for the anthology. A young girl named Letha meets a boy at her parents' annual summer solstice bonfire.

I dreamed about it that night.

I could smell the smoke from the bonfire and hear the wood crackle. In my dream, it was in my backyard, which was much bigger than it really was.

Letha was watching the flames when the boy sat down next to her. He said, "Where have you been? I've been looking for you everywhere."

She said, "I've been waiting all this time for you to see me."

Most of the time, when I dream about a book I'm working on, I wake up feeling invigorated and ready to try to capture the scene. It's as if when my conscious mind is turned off, my unconscious mind gets a chance to play and thoroughly enjoys it.

But the next day, rather than invigorated, that dream left me feeling . . . unsettled. All day long, the feeling hovered over me, even as the story flew from my fingers to the laptop screen.

I tried to push the feeling aside as I finished getting dressed for my date with Anthony. I'd wanted to stay in and order pizza, but he'd already made arrangements to have dinner at the Johnsons', his partners and Ned's bosses.

It grated a bit that he hadn't bothered to ask me. I was unaccustomed to someone making plans for me without at least checking with me beforehand.

It seemed . . . cheeky.

I'd said as much to Anthony. He'd been thoroughly mystified about why I'd been annoyed that he'd just assumed I'd be thrilled. I agreed to go, but I wasn't happy about it.

It wasn't that I didn't like the Johnsons. I did.

And, as I suspect, it was a nice dinner. Josiah and Muriel were a great couple. But Ned had been right. They didn't actually fight, but they squabbled . . . a lot. They squabbled about weird legal facts that I didn't even begin to understand.

They squabbled about the proper way to prepare a steak.

They squabbled about who came up with some new strategy for a case and then spent a great deal of time discussing it with Anthony.

Some people might have been upset to have people conversing about topics that they couldn't contribute to, but frankly, I enjoyed watching the two of them. I'll confess, I blatantly studied how they interacted with each other.

Josiah and Muriel were each absolutely convinced that his or her opinion was the correct one. They lived in this black-and-white world. Right and wrong. Their way or the highway.

I'd spent my life living in a gray realm, where the only absolute was there was no absolute. Every rule had an exception. Every situation had multiple outcomes.

Anthony joined in the fracas on occasion.

I was a bystander, but I liked watching how all three of them thought. Anthony was a step-one-then-step-two sort of thinker. He seemed to get thrown if someone interrupted that process.

Muriel was a jackrabbit, hopping from one tangent to another, then hopping back again.

And Josiah was . . . a quoter. He cited books and articles to back up his points.

To be honest, I had no idea what points they were each making most of the time, but it was fascinating listening to them all. Stepping, quoting, and hopping around a case.

"We're being rude," Muriel finally said. Both men stopped talking and she continued, "I'm sorry, Piper. If you put a bunch of lawyers together, this is what happens."

I shook my head. "Really, I was enjoying the conversation. Watching how you all thought and formulated your arguments was fascinating."

"Uh-oh," Anthony teased. "We've been together long enough for me to know that means we're all about to become fodder for Piper's next book."

"No. Not any of you in specific. But watching your thought processes—how different they all were—might inspire something in the future. Now, if I were John Grisham, your actual arguments might have been of more use, since he writes so much legal fiction. When you're writing about teens, legal facts aren't normally required."

"If Grisham had been here, he'd have joined in the debates," Muriel assured me. "Most attorneys can't resist a good fight."

The rest of the evening the topics were ones I could contribute to, though their lawyerly love of arguments continued to show through as we all debated *Star Trek* versus *Star Wars*. I loved both, Anthony loved neither, Muriel was *Star Trek,* and Josiah was *Star Wars.*

The lines were fairly well drawn.

I was still laughing about it when Anthony pulled his car into my drive. "I don't believe I've ever been involved in such a fierce fight," I said.

"I didn't realize they were both such fans of the genre." He added, "I'm sorry for springing the dinner on you."

"I don't do springing very well," I told him. "Next time ask first?"

He nodded. "I've never been involved with someone for this long. I obviously don't have much experience in what's appropriate."

"Even if we're together thirty years from now, asking first would be the way to go."

"Wow, our first fight," he said with a chuckle. "I think we weathered it fairly well."

"No, I'm pretty sure the *Star Wars, Star Trek* debate has to count as our first fight. Even if it doesn't, let's say it was because it will make a more interesting story in the future."

"You're right about that," he said with a hint of laughter in his voice. "Two fights in one night and we survived."

"We did."

He leaned over and kissed me. When he drew back he said, "I'd ask to come in, but I've got to be at court first thing in the morning."

"No problem. I'll talk to you soon." That was the nice thing about dating Anthony. We both respected each other's schedules.

I opened my door but Ned called out, "Hey," before I went in.

"Hey, yourself," I called back and let the door slam shut. I waited and Ned came over and joined me on the porch. "How was your date?"

"Nice. We were at Muriel and Josiah's."

"A gaggle of lawyers at dinner." He shook his head. "I bet that made for some interesting conversations."

"Well, there was some lawyerly talk. And by *talk* I mean debates. They were out of my league. But then they discussed science fiction."

"And you held your own in that arena," he said with a surety that came from knowing and sharing my love of the genre.

"Oh, I did," I assured him.

"I thought Anthony wasn't a fan of science fiction," he said.

We'd invited Anthony to some of our opening night shows, but he'd always declined. I'm not sure if Ned had ever invited Mela. She hadn't been a fan of the genre, but I suspected that if he'd invited her, she'd have come.

I worried about Ned since he broke things off with Mela. He hadn't gone on any other dates, as far as I knew. He'd been alone for a couple months now. Maybe he'd come out because he was lonely.

I nodded at the chairs, and we both took a seat. "Anthony's not a fan, but turns out the Johnsons are . . ."

We sat on my porch, under the glow of the light from the school-yard, and talked about *Star Trek* versus *Star Wars*. Then we discussed which *Star Trek* franchises we liked best.

I'm not sure how long we sat there, talking in the murky light that filtered through my serviceberry trees, but Ned finally said, "I should let you get to bed."

"How about you? Are you going to be able to get some sleep tonight?" I'd noticed a light on in his living room a lot at night since Mela broke up with him.

"I think I will," he told me.

"Good."

I watched him go inside and waved as he shut the door. I was worried about him. Even when you know a decision is for the best, it can still hurt.

I wished there was something I could do to make it easier on him.

I sat outside a while longer, looking at the light spilling from his living room window. I tried to think of something I could do.

Anything.

But in the end, I had to admit certain hurts simply needed time in order to heal.

And certain hurts, no matter how long you waited, never fully healed.

⚓ ⚓ ⚓

That Saturday was an Amanda's Pantry Saturday. This week, Ned had volunteered to come help. We hadn't talked about Mela, but he still seemed out of sorts. I'd spent the day trying to make him smile, and I thought I'd done a pretty good job of lightening his mood.

It wasn't hard for me to be happy on Amanda's Pantry days. I loved interacting with our clients. Our last client of the day was Mimi Ridley. She always brought her daughter, Lovey, with her. Lovey wasn't actually her name. It was Lisbeth. But once you met her, you never had any doubt that her true name was Lovey.

Lovey came in and crawled on my lap. She was tiny for a kindergartener and fit on it with ease. "I made you somethin'." Without waiting for me to ask what, she thrust a small stack of papers in my hand. "I wrote you a book 'cause you gave me some and I wanted to give you some back."

"Lovey, that was so sweet of you." There were colorful but hard-to-identify pictures and random letters filling the pages. "Would you read it to me?"

"Sure," she said as she nodded like a bobblehead doll. "Once upon a time, there was Miss Pip and she told stories." She pointed to a picture. "That's you and a book and me and some other kids."

I nodded as if that's exactly what the circles and squiggles meant to me.

"And she gives them food, and last time, she gave Lovey some stuff for pancakes." She pointed to ovals on the next page. "That's me eatin' pancakes. Mom made 'em for me."

"That was nice of your mom," I assured her.

"And that's me and Mom after we ate them." The ovals had morphed into broad circles.

"That's lovely, Lovey." The pictures might be a bit hard to identify, but the heart of the story was there, and it was a beautiful heart.

"I wanted to bring you some, but Mom said they'd be cold, and cold pancakes aren't good."

Ned stepped up. "That's okay. I was going to take Miss Pip out tomorrow for pancakes."

"You were?" she asked, her eyes wide, as if she were amazed by Ned's mind-reading skills.

Ned nodded, completely serious. "Yes. I was going to ask her if she'd come with me and help me find a dog tomorrow, and I thought I'd feed her pancakes first." He leaned close and whispered, "When you ask someone for a favor, it's a good idea to do something nice for them first."

Lovey weighed his words and nodded enthusiastically. "Yeah, that is a good idea. What kind of dog you gettin'?"

"That's my problem." He sighed as if that very question had weighed on him heavily. "I don't know what kind. Ms. Pip is good at figuring out people, so I thought she might help me decide just what kind of dog I need. I think choosing a dog is an important decision."

"Yeah, that's important. I bet she could help you. She likes to help people."

Ned grinned at me, and I felt warmed by his expression. Ned's happiness had come to mean a lot to me.

He whispered to Lovey again, as if her mom and I couldn't hear him. "She does like to help them a lot."

"Will you bring the dog with you sometime?" Lovey asked.

"I'll tell you what, if you and your mom can come at the end of the day in two weeks, I'll come and I'll bring my dog with me. I'm not sure he'll want to be here for a whole day, but I bet he'd like to walk over for a visit."

Lovey turned around and asked Mimi. "Mom?"

Mimi nodded. "We always come late because I work Saturdays until two."

"And I go stay with Mrs. Sandy across the street." Lovey dropped her voice to a stage whisper and announced, "And she makes me lunches, but she don't never make me pancakes."

I had never seen Ned interact with a child before. Oh, he'd helped at the food pantry before and he'd certainly talked to kids, but not like this. There was a connection between him and Lovely. He was good with her.

I realized that in all the time we'd dated, Anthony had never come down to the food pantry and helped. Even knowing how much it meant to me.

I tried to tell myself that I'd never gone to court to help him with a case, but I knew it wasn't the same thing.

Ned and Lovey chatted about dogs and pancakes as I helped Mimi.

And when they left, Lovey hugged Ned and promised to bring him his own book in two weeks.

卍 卍 卍

The next morning, after the promised breakfast of pancakes, Ned and I went to the Everything But a Dog adoption event. It was held at the amphitheater down on the bay front.

I loved it on the bay. The area used to be an industrial hub for Erie, but over the last decade or so, industries had left and hotels, the main library, and tourist attractions had moved in.

From the rise, I could see down the grassy knoll to the amphitheater itself, and beyond that, the bay and Presque Isle peninsula on the far side.

Sailboats, motorboats, and kayaks dotted the bay water. Most days, looking at it would be enough of a reason to visit Liberty Park, but today we were here on a mission.

"Are you ready?" I asked Ned.

He nodded.

We began to walk through the park. There were dogs of every size and breed, in kennels and makeshift pens.

"How did you find out about this?" I asked as we walked aimlessly through rows of dogs.

I'll confess that part of me wanted to take each and every one of the dogs home with me. Some looked excited to be out of the shelter; some looked depressed. All of them looked like they needed a home.

"Josiah knows the Salo family who runs this," Ned said. "Well, he said it's actually the matriarch of the family who runs the organization and she enlists the rest of the family. According to Josiah, they don't really have a choice."

Mrs. Salo sounded bossy. And that thought, coupled with the mention of Josiah, reminded me about Anthony's making plans for us.

"Where do the dogs come from?" I asked, rather than dwell on Anthony's faux pas.

"All the shelters in town send the dogs over. The lady, Mrs. Salo, claims to have a special power to match dogs to the right owner."

I laughed at the thought of a matchmaker who specialized in dogs.

Ned smiled. "Yeah, I have my doubts about her, but not about you. I trust you to help me find the right dog."

"I've never had a dog, so I have no idea what to suggest when you're looking for one."

"You have insight, Pip. You have an ability to see inside people." Ned knelt down by a houndish-looking dog. It sniffed his hand, then left him to go visit with a couple kids who'd come over.

"Not that one," I said with a laugh.

He nodded and moved to the next pen. "I think your insight into people is why you're so good at what you do. I'm good at digging up facts and measurable information about people, but you get to the heart of them."

It was a lovely compliment. I sometimes wanted to argue when people said nice things about me or my work, but my agent had taught me that there were only two words necessary after any compliment.

"Thank you," I said, following her advice. Then I asked, "So why a dog now?"

Ned shrugged and I thought that was all the answer I was going to get, but finally he said, "Mela never liked dogs. She didn't want the hair all over and she said they smelled. I don't have to worry about that anymore, so I'm getting a dog."

I didn't want to talk about Mela. I was afraid that the fact we never liked each other would show through, so instead I asked, "Do you have a breed in mind?"

He shook his head. "Just a dog. I had a mutt when I was growing up. Major. He was supposed to be my father's dog, but it was apparent from the get-go he was mine. Or maybe it would be more correct to say I was his. I think in most cases, the dog owns the human . . . it doesn't matter if the human in question realizes it."

A tiny little woman who had reached a point in her life where it was hard to assign a number to her age, said, "Oh, isn't that the truth? My dogs, now they own me and I know it, but some people never do. My husband, he didn't want dogs, but now they own him, too. He doesn't know it, but me and the dogs do." She eyed us up for a long moment, not saying anything, but studying us.

As she studied us, I studied her. She would make a wonderful grandmother in a book. She was so tiny that most of my preteen characters would be able to lift her, but she had that sort of indomitable aura that would mean none of my characters would ever dare.

She gave a little nod, more to herself than to us and said, "I have your dogs right over here." She didn't wait for a response but started walking down a row of makeshift dog pens, trusting we'd follow.

"Dog," I corrected as we followed her because . . . well, it seemed like the thing to do. "Ned's here for the dog. I'm just advising. So dog . . . singular."

For a tiny woman she had a very large laugh. Without turning around she said, "No, you're here for a dog. You just don't know it yet."

Before I could argue, she stopped in front of a kennel with two dogs. "This is Princess and Bruce."

Princess was a tall dog with a poodle-ish look, but had wild, whitish hair that zigzagged in weird ringlets all over her body. Bruce was some kind of hound dog that didn't bother to look up when we approached.

"I'll let you all get to know each other," the woman said and moved toward another couple farther down the row.

"Well, that was different," I said.

Ned didn't respond. He was watching the dogs with an intensity that didn't leave room for anything else.

Princess was doing a pretty little dance of happiness as Ned reached over the barricade to pet her. She wiggled as if her glee was so vast she had to do something to let some of it out.

After lapping up Ned's attention, Princess went back over to Bruce and nudged him to his feet. She walked back to us, trusting that he would follow, rather like the old lady who'd led us to this pen. Princess ignored me and went back to Ned, her preference clear. Bruce slowly ambled over to me and simply looked at me.

He had such sad eyes.

Big, droopy eyes that said, *I expect nothing from life so I'm rarely disappointed.*

I held out my hand and he licked it. I patted his head and he gave a halfhearted tail wag, as if he wanted to let me know he liked me, but he still had no expectations about our relationship.

The woman who had to be the matriarch running the event, Mrs. Salo, was suddenly back at our sides. "See, I told you," she said. "Princess was waiting for him, and Bruce here was just waiting for you."

Having decided she'd settled things for the two of us and the dogs, she walked in the opposite direction, this time to a family near the entrance.

"Well . . ." I said. Bruce didn't wiggle or do a gleeful happy dance like Princess, but I could see that he enjoyed my attention.

"*Well* is right. She was an original," Ned agreed. "But I think she might be right even though Princess isn't the type of dog I imagined myself with."

As if she realized that he was talking about her, Princess jumped up, reached over the fence, and put her paws on his shoulders. Her head was just beneath his chin and she gazed at him adoringly.

"You might not have imagined yourself with Princess, but she obviously has made her choice of princes known." I didn't need to be an expert about dogs, or be someone with empathetic insights into people, to see that Ned and Princess were meant for each other.

"And you?" he asked. "You didn't come here to get a dog, but if you decide to take him home, you know I'll help out."

Bruce looked at me as if to say, *It's all right. I know you don't want a dog.*

The thing is, I discovered I did very much want a dog. Not just any dog, *this* dog.

I nodded at Ned. "Yes, he's mine. And thanks. You know I'll help with Princess, too."

We filled out the paperwork and an hour later, we were walking our dogs down along the bay front.

"Look." Among the other boats the Brig *Niagara* floated by. Once it had been the flagship of the Battle of Lake Erie; now it was the emissary of Erie. The rebuilt replica traveled ports all along the Great Lakes and was one of Erie's crowning jewels. I could see the people sprinkled along the deck. "It's probably one of its day sails. They take people out in the bay and onto the lake itself. Have you ever gone on one?"

Ned shook his head.

"I did once," I told him.

The dogs seemed thoroughly unimpressed with the ship.

Princess was still prancing around. It was as if she found the entire world was full of wonder and she couldn't contain herself. Bruce seemed as taciturn as he had at the event. Though I thought he did seem to have a bit more optimism in his step.

"What do you think Anthony's going to say when he finds out you have a dog?"

"Congratulations? I mean, what else could he say?"

"He's over an awful lot. He might not be any more enamored of dogs than Mela was."

"While I like and enjoy Anthony's company, I would never make a decision about my life around him and his desires."

As I said the words, it struck me that if Anthony and I were truly a couple, I *would* make decisions based on him. I pushed the thought away.

We all took a trip to the local pet center and Princess and Bruce were soon decked out with every possible doggie decadence.

ૐ ૐ ૐ

Anthony came over that night. "Surprise," I said, pointing to Bruce, who'd decided the rug in front of my fireplace was more comfortable than the dog bed I'd bought for him.

Anthony looked at Bruce. "Whose dog is that?"

"My dog."

Anthony wrinkled his nose as if Bruce smelled, which I know he didn't because I'd bathed him after we got home. "Oh."

"Aren't you going to say congratulations?" I asked.

"I'm going to confess, I am not a dog lover," he said slowly.

I couldn't hold that against him since I'd never thought about getting a dog until today. "He'll grow on you."

Anthony didn't look convinced. "I wish you would have talked to me about it."

It was on the tip of my tongue to say *why would I?* but that seemed rude, so I settled for saying, "I didn't plan on him, but I'm glad he's here."

Anthony simply nodded.

I hadn't had a lot of experience functioning as half of a couple. Maybe I should have mentioned getting a dog to Anthony.

In the end, I decided no, I shouldn't have.

We were dating, not engaged or married.

I didn't need to ask his permission. After all, I was making a decision for myself, not for both of us.

Anthony left rather early. He'd wanted to go out, but I didn't want to leave Bruce alone his first night home.

Not that I thought Bruce would have been overly bothered at being left. He seemed at home at my place and content to curl up on the rug.

When I went out to the front porch, he happily came along and curled up on the loveseat as I wrote in Amanda's journal.

> *Dear Amanda,*
>
> *I wonder if you have a pet.*
>
> *I never did. It never occurred to me to want one, but now that I have Bruce, I can't imagine not having him.*
>
> *I'd have never thought about getting a pet on my own, but thanks to Ned, I have one.*
>
> *Maybe that's what having a good friend is all about . . . having someone who pushes you to try new things and forces you to look at the world in a new way.*
>
> *I love the scene in Dead Poets Society where Robin Williams gets up on a desk and tells his students to look at the world from a new perspective.*
>
> *When I looked at Bruce sleeping on the rug in front of the fireplace earlier, and now, as he's curled up on the loveseat, I can see that I was always meant to have a dog . . . I just didn't know it until Ned showed me that*

I did. Now, I'm on top of Robin Williams' desk, looking at my life from a different perspective, and I realize I was always meant to have a dog . . . this dog.

I hope you have a pet, too. If not, I hope when you're older, you get one.

Love,
Piper

Junior Year

Chapter Nine

Thanksgiving's a crazy time for me. We gear up at Amanda's Pantry, try-ing to make sure everyone who uses our services has the ingredients for a proper holiday meal. All our volunteers show up to hand out baskets the weekend before.

Ned, my parents, and Cooper were there this year.

Anthony was not.

He was involved in a big case and said he didn't have the time.

I tried not to let it bother me, but it did. He'd still never come to the food pantry. I was on my way to Thanksgiving at his parents' place in Pittsburgh, because it was important to him. But I'd never felt he placed any priority on what was important to me.

Little things. I kept trying to tell myself that I couldn't let the little things wear away at what was a good, comfortable relationship, but they did.

Just a few weeks ago, Anthony called and invited me to lunch with him, Josiah, and Muriel. I said I would have loved to join them, but I was working.

He laughed and said I could do that as easily before lunch as after.

Later in the conversation he said something about me just sitting around my house with my dog.

He still didn't like Bruce.

I'm not sure why I was thinking about that as we headed down I-79 toward Pittsburgh. As much as I tried to tamp down the feelings of being underappreciated, they kept swirling around my thoughts.

I wanted Anthony to understand that my work and Amanda's Pantry were as important to me as his work was to him. I wanted him to be involved in my life and passions. I'd joined him for a number of other parties and gatherings because they were important to him. I didn't feel the consideration was reciprocated.

I tried to hold back a sigh because I was back to feeling annoyed about him skipping out on Amanda's Pantry. To be honest, I hadn't told him about Amanda, but even without knowing about her, the food pantry was obviously something I felt passionate about.

The question nagged at me. Why hadn't I told him about Amanda?

It wasn't embarrassment that I'd been a teen parent. Amanda was my heart. She was at the very core of everything I'd done since she was born. Maybe the reason I didn't talk about her was that sharing my heart didn't come easily.

I'd sent such a large piece of my heart away with her that maybe I simply safeguarded what was left.

I had not planned on making the drive to Pittsburgh for Thanksgiving, but again Anthony simply assumed I'd go with him. I chafed at his making plans for us, as if we were joined at the hip and functioned as a pair. But I'd gone because it was important to him. He'd shared holidays with my family, so it seemed fair I share one with his.

Ned volunteered to take Bruce for the day and teased about the massive holiday dinner he was going to make the dogs.

I'd never spent a holiday away from my parents. They decided to go out to dinner instead of cooking. Maybe my mother would enjoy the break.

Still, it felt wrong not to be at home.

Most years Mom and I did most of the meal preparations.

Except the turkey. Dad was not a cook, but brining a turkey was his one cooking expertise. For more than a decade now, he brined them, then stuffed and prepped them. Each year he experimented with the brine. Last year he used an apple wine in it . . . it added a little something delicious to the taste.

Dad said as long as a man could excel at one dish, the rest was gravy. Then he always added the word *literally* and laughed. It really wasn't funny, but we always laughed, too.

Once the prep was done, we had another family tradition. We pulled out *White Christmas* and picked at leftovers as we watched Bing, Danny, Rosemary, and Vera dance and sing . . . and fall in love.

"You're very quiet," Anthony said, and without waiting to give me a chance to respond, he added, "We're almost there."

The tree-lined sections of I-79 gave way to city views. And finally, he turned off the highway all together and made his way to his family's Squirrel Hill neighborhood. He pulled up in front of a lovely brick home in the middle of a cul-de-sac. "This is where you grew up?"

"Yes. It's considered a classic revival." He laughed. "I'm not sure precisely what that means, but my stepmother will probably explain it to you at length, whether or not you want to know."

"I love to talk about things like that," I said as I got out of the car and smoothed down my dress.

"Did I mention how nice you look today?" Anthony asked. "You should make some effort more often."

He leaned down and kissed me.

I felt nothing but another spurt of annoyance and I knew that wasn't fair. I'd dressed up, hoping to make a good impression on his father and stepmother. That Anthony had noticed and appreciated the attempt shouldn't have bugged me, but it did.

His parents were delightful, and some of the vexation I knew I'd been stoking faded.

His stepmother, Anne, was a petite brunette with a large smile and bubbly personality. His father was also named Anthony, but there was no confusion since Anthony and his stepmother both referred to Anthony's father as *the judge*.

Dinner was a catered affair. It arrived at two o'clock from a local restaurant. I helped Anne put everything into serving dishes.

The four of us sat in a formal dining room with hardwood floors, dark wood trim, and a stained glass transom that ran above the windows.

It was the kind of meal that required multiple forks.

The judge and Anthony talked about cases and trials for a while. When there was a break in that conversation, I asked Anne about the house. She talked about meeting the judge because of her work for a preservation society.

Anthony said, "Piper does a lot of volunteer work as well."

"And you're a writer, correct?" the judge asked.

"Yes. I volunteer for a local food pantry—"

Anthony interrupted. "She's being modest. She started it and runs it. And she reads to kids at the school across from her house."

"Oh, that's nice," said Anne.

"They're my audience. It's a nice way to try out new material," I said, feeling uncomfortable.

"You write children's books?" Anne asked.

I nodded.

"The volunteering and children's books . . . those are the kinds of things that are very marketable for a man who has political aspirations," the judge said in such a way that I suspected that Anthony had some political aspirations I'd never heard of.

"Just throw in a kissable baby and there's no race that can't be won," Anne said with a laugh.

"Unless the baby barfs or cries," I pointed out.

Three sets of eyes shot me looks that said clearly that in their world babies did not barf, at least not as a matter of dinner table conversation. I took a long drink, hoping to cover my embarrassment.

"Speaking of babies," Anne said, steering away from my faux pas. "I know I won't be their real grandmother, but I'd do my best to spoil them rotten when you and Anthony . . ."

She let her words die off as I started to choke on my drink. When I stopped my spastic coughing, I said, "There are no babies in my future."

She changed the topic once again and we finished dinner, but I'd seen Anthony's expression.

After dinner, I helped Anne with the dishes while the men discussed more cases. Then we regrouped and continued discussing . . . legal issues and added a few political things into the mix. Every time I tried to steer the conversation to something that was more group friendly, the gambit fell with a thud.

I tried not to compare the experience with the thought of sitting at my parents' watching *White Christmas*, but I'm afraid I did. And Anthony's holiday, by comparison, was lacking.

On the ride home, he said, "About kids. You don't want them or you can't have them?"

"Does it matter? Kids are not in my future." Now. Now would be the time to tell him about Amanda and explain. I tried to push the words out past the huge lump in my throat, but couldn't manage it.

"We could adopt," he said.

I didn't know what to say. We'd been dating a year, and I guess that's why Anthony had begun thinking beyond simply dating. But I . . . I hadn't. At least not about the two of us.

I'd never felt as if we were close enough to have a discussion about hypothetical children, but then I never felt we were close enough for Anthony to assume we functioned as a unit and he could speak for me.

"Anthony, I am not planning to have children, biological or adopted," I said as clearly and succinctly as I knew how.

"Why? You're so good with kids. You make your living dealing with kids. I've never read your books, but I've looked at them online. The reviews all talk about how you understand your audience."

"I guess in a way, I have a lot of children already. Every book I write is like a child. I take it from conception to book. And then I turn it over to the readers, and in another way, they're my children, too. I don't need anything more than that."

"I do," he said slowly.

"I'm sorry," I said.

The conversation fizzled after that.

I knew I should tell Anthony about Amanda. If I explained, he might understand. But I couldn't. I'd always known that if I ever fell for someone, I would tell him about the daughter I'd given away.

The fact that I couldn't share this with Anthony was telling.

And I was pretty sure exactly what it was telling me, but I didn't act on it because I wasn't truly ready to admit it. I thought maybe if I gave it some time, we'd figure our way around the issue. Maybe if I gave it more time, my feelings would change.

When we pulled in my driveway, Anthony kissed me and said he had a lot of work the next day, so he was heading home.

It was late, after midnight, and though I wanted Bruce back, I wasn't going to wake up Ned in order to get him.

After Anthony pulled away, I realized I was too wired to go to bed, so I went out to my porch.

I thought about getting Amanda's journal.

I'd found that sometimes writing to her helped me clarify things in my own mind. Maybe if I explained my reluctance to tell Anthony about her on the journal's pages, I could make sense of it all.

After all, Anthony was a nice man. We'd been dating a year now, and I enjoyed his company, even if I occasionally bristled at his heavy-handedness lately.

Part of that was my fault. I'd let him. I was going to have to say something.

As nice as his father and stepmother were, I missed being home, surrounded by my family.

I knew that wasn't fair. When two people were in a relationship, there had to be some give-and-take. Maybe the fact that I resented spending the holiday with his family made me selfish.

Maybe not wanting to have more children made me selfish, too.

And not explaining Amanda to Anthony, that more than anything probably made me selfish. I held onto her, unwilling to share her with anyone else.

I never spoke of her to my parents, who knew about her, or my friends, who didn't.

It wasn't from embarrassment or even pain.

I stared at the empty school. Most nights, lights glowed from windows as the cleaning crew worked. But tonight was a holiday and it was empty and dark.

Maybe that's why I didn't talk about Amanda.

I was afraid if I shared her, only emptiness would remain, so I clung to the moments that I had, hoarding them like some miser who was unwilling to share the wealth.

I *was* selfish.

"Penny for your thoughts," said Ned, interrupting my self-examination.

Bruce and Princess greeted me with more enthusiasm than manners. "I missed you, too," I assured both dogs.

"I was just going to take them for a quick walk before bed," Ned explained. "Want to join us?"

"Sure. Let me change shoes." I ran back inside, kicked off my heels, and slipped on a pair of sneakers. "These look absurd with the dress," I said when I came back out, "but I wouldn't have made it much past your house in the heels."

"That's fine with me. You always look a bit . . . well, 'not you' in dressy clothes. I mean, you look nice and all, but I'm used to you . . ." Ned stopped. "I'm making a mess of what was supposed to be reassurance."

"No, I took it as a compliment." It felt nice to have someone think I looked okay when I was dressed in my regular clothes. "I never quite feel like myself in dressy clothes. I'm more at home in my jeans, a laptop balanced on my thighs, or out in the backyard planting something new."

"Sipping out of your fancy teacup and talking to the voices in your head." Laughter tinged his voice.

I smiled as we walked along in companionable silence. The dogs paused every now and then to sniff some fascinating smell or do what dogs did on walks.

"So, why were you heading out walking so late?" I asked.

"I was on the job and just got home a bit before you must have."

"You worked on Thanksgiving?" I asked.

"We have a witness who has been . . . well, not easy to find. I figured he'd find it hard to stay away from his family during the holiday. Most people want to be home. And I was right. He showed up at his parents' and I tailed him back to his new address."

"Definitely a *Magnum, PI* move," I teased.

He laughed. "So how did 'meet the parents' go?"

"They were very nice." It was a noncommittal response. I was afraid that Ned would push and I'd have to say the words I was just beginning to suspect.

I should have known better. Ned never pushed me.

We walked in silence. The dogs were leash trained when we'd adopted them, so walking was easy with them.

I'd always thought that autumn smelled of cinnamon. I breathed deeply and decided winter smelled of peppermint. Not peppermint candy, but the real herb I had growing in the backyard. Sharp, cold, with a bit of a bite. Clean. Not that it was officially winter yet, but the season arrives early on the shore of Lake Erie.

As if on cue, it started to snow.

"And thus it begins," Ned intoned.

I laughed. "Another Erie winter."

"Snow shovels and snowblowers," he said.

I added, "Snow brushes."

Ned took it as a challenge, thought a moment and said, "Snow pants."

"Come on, that's a bit of a cheat. When's the last time you wore snow pants?"

"Last time I went skiing at Peek'n Peak with Mela," he said.

He hadn't mentioned her in a long time. "Do you miss her?"

Ned shook his head. "No. I thought maybe, if nothing else, I'd miss the companionship, but it's been six months and I don't. That seems harsh to say." He sighed. "I do feel her absence sometimes, but it's not quite missing and more of a passing thought than a heartache, if that makes sense. And now that I have Princess, the house seems full enough."

I nodded. I understood that. I'd always been someone comfortable being by myself. Even as a child. Give me a book and a comfortable chair and I could make an entire day of it.

Other people needed people. I couldn't imagine my mom without my dad. Even the judge and Anne seemed to . . . well, fit. Josiah and Muriel, too.

Ned and Mela? Obviously not.

And Anthony and me?

I knew the answer, but I wasn't ready to face it.

Ned and I walked, in the peppermint-scented snow, and I wondered if I was one of those people who were simply meant to be alone.

⚜ ⚜ ⚜

I pondered my relationship with Anthony for the next two weeks. The annual snowstorms began arriving in earnest. Band after band of cold

Canadian air blew over our warmer great lake, picking up moisture. When it reached land, it dumped not inches of snow but feet.

The back garden became a winter fairyland. Snow coated the branches. My birdbath froze over, and every day I trudged along the packed-down path and melted the ice and replaced it with water before I filled the feeders.

Some days, when the weather wasn't too harsh, I walked through the snow-covered garden, enjoying the starkness that was so different from the lushness in summer . . . different but equally beautiful.

I missed writing on my porch, but truthfully, the chair by the window was only a foot from where I normally sat. It was a Stickley chair and I swear they designed it for me to write from.

From my seat I could still watch the rhythm of my neighborhood. I watched school begin, then end each day. Kids arrive and depart. I saw delivery people drive by and occasionally stop.

Being inside served to separate me from everyone else. I felt more removed, and the world seemed much quieter than it felt in other seasons.

In that silence, there was nothing for me to do but think.

I saw very little of Anthony. He was busy with a case; I was busy with a deadline. When he did come over, we didn't talk about Thanksgiving or children. We also didn't speak about what I now suspected were his political ambitions.

Moving to a new city as a partner in a law firm. That might have been a strategic business move, or it might have been the first step in a political career.

The subjects we didn't speak of added to the wall that was growing between us. Each visit, it became more apparent and harder to ignore.

Ned had been busy with work, too. I wondered if he was investigating things for Anthony's case, but he didn't say and I didn't ask. I just knew that he left his house early, so most mornings, I went over, got

Princess, and walked the dogs together. But without Ned's company, I had even more time to think.

Normally I'd be thinking about whatever book I was working on—my work-in-progress. Or I'd be thinking about Amanda's Pantry. But now, all my thoughts were on Anthony as I tried to work out what I should do.

When I was totally honest with myself, I acknowledged I didn't need to work out what I should do. I was working out how to accept it. How to accept that I'd spent a year with a man I didn't love.

The week before Christmas, Anthony called and asked if he could come over. It was a very formal request, especially coming from a man who more than once had made decisions on both our behalves.

As I waited for him, I realized there was no sense of anticipation. I hadn't missed him. All the little snippets of thought that had skittered around the fringes of my awareness landed with a thud.

I thought about what Ned had said about Mela. He could picture his life without her.

I didn't want to admit it, but I couldn't avoid the realization any longer . . . I felt that way about Anthony. I could picture my life without him in it.

And I knew what I had to do. Or rather, I admitted what I'd known for some time.

When I met Anthony, there'd been no spark. But he was nice and I thought that warmth was just as good as full-out flame.

The two of us would have been good friends, but we'd tried for something else. But it's hard to find something that was never there in the first place.

We'd been seeing each other for over a year and I knew that we would never be any closer than we were now.

That wasn't fair to Anthony, and it wasn't fair to me.

I couldn't decide if I should tell him after dinner or before.

I decided to make a salad and have it in the fridge.

He arrived promptly at six. "I thought I was going to be late." He was bouncy happy and carrying a bottle of wine, which he thrust in my direction. "The verdict came in. Not guilty."

"Congratulations," I said and meant it.

"Thanks. I know that the case took a lot of time away from us. We never really talked about Thanksgiving and . . ."

Part of me—a part I'm not very proud of—wanted to forget about breaking up with him tonight. He was so happy. It was unkind dumping news like this on him. And it wasn't as if I didn't like him. I did. We'd been dating for a year. What were a few more days?

A lie.

"Anthony, we need to talk."

His happy expression melted away. "So this is it?"

"Could we sit down?"

He nodded. We sat on the couch. Anthony on one side, me on the other. There was an entire empty cushion between us.

I thought that pretty much summed up our relationship.

"I had a dream a while ago. It started out as a scene for my new story. It was about a midsummer's celebration. A bonfire. I don't think we've ever had a bonfire, or even a spark between us. Anthony, we don't belong together."

"I thought with time . . ." He let the sentence die off.

He didn't need to go on, because I knew just what he was saying. "Me, too. I like you. And I care about you. But we both want different things."

"Kids," he said.

I nodded. "Yes."

"I thought you might change your mind on that as well."

I shook my head. "It's more than just that one issue. When we spend time apart, we both seem comfortable with it. We both seem to get along just fine without the other. Maybe I think we both deserve to be with people we can't stand to be apart from."

He nodded. "I'll confess, I was relieved that you didn't kick up a fuss when I was spending so much time on this case. I'd had other girl-friends who weren't so understanding."

"And I was happy to have uninterrupted time to work on a book." Maybe if I were completely on my own, it would have been different. But Cooper and Ned had both been around. And my parents were always there. My life still felt well populated with people without Anthony around.

I think that was the point. If I were with someone I truly loved, even if my life were filled to capacity, I'd still feel the lack of his presence.

"So we're over." Anthony made it a statement more than a question.

I nodded and spanned that no-man's-land cushion and took his hand. "I think we both deserve to find people we can't live without. People we can't be apart from because it causes an almost physical pain. People who know us inside and out and like us anyway."

He nodded, but didn't say anything.

"I'm sorry it took me so long to say something. I had an inkling last Christmas."

"What happened last Christmas?" he asked.

"I was living in terror you'd want me to go to that hockey game with you," I confessed with a laugh.

He gave a little halfhearted chuckle, then said, "I guess I can con-fess that I worried you'd want to come. I knew you didn't like hockey. But at least you came up with the idea for a perfect gift. I didn't have a clue, and while I did notice that your copy of *Have Space Suit—Will Travel* was worn, I only noticed after Ned gave me the idea. I was think-ing I was going to have to ask him for a suggestion for this year, too."

I laughed. I should have known it was Ned, my sci-fi buddy, who realized how much I loved that book. "I had the idea of giving you some sporty sort of gift, but Ned was the one who told me the team and game."

"So what you're saying is Ned knows us better than we know each other?" Anthony half joked.

Only half, because I think he realized that there was a lot of truth in that statement.

I thought about Anthony's comment about my clothing on Thanksgiving. He wished I'd make an effort more often. Ned had said he liked me in my normal mode of dress.

Yes, Ned knew more about me than just my love of science fiction. The thought made me uncomfortable, so I brushed it aside and concentrated on Anthony.

"So we're okay?" I asked. "I mean, I hope I see you at the annual Amanda's Pantry dinner along with the rest of the firm. I don't want things between us to be . . . weird."

He smiled. "I've never had an ex who worried about us being okay after a breakup. But then you've never been an average girlfriend, so the fact you're going to be a non-average ex makes sense. But to be clear, yes, we're fine."

"If I ever need a lawyer, I'd call you," I said and I meant it. I had complete faith that if I ever needed help and asked, Anthony would come running.

He smiled. "Well, of course you would. After all, I just won a big case. I'm good."

I looked at Anthony and realized he was a friend.

I don't know how I could have thought he was anything more than that, but I knew for a fact he wasn't anything less. And when we met in the future at dinners or just around town, I knew I'd always be genuinely happy to see him and anxious to catch up.

"So, would it be weird if I asked you to stay for dinner after I broke up with you?" I asked.

There was no halfhearted smile or small chuckle. Anthony shook his head, rolled his eyes, and genuinely laughed. "Yes, but Piper, we've been together for a year . . . I've gotten used to your weirdness." He paused. "Maybe that sums us up. I've gotten used to you; you've gotten used to me. But just because we're accustomed to each other doesn't mean we're in love."

"No, it doesn't. But it does mean we can be friends?" I said more than asked.

He nodded. "Absolutely."

We had the wine he'd brought and my salad. He told me all about his case and I told him about my book.

We talked and laughed.

And that's when I realized how relieved I was that I wasn't going to lose his friendship.

Maybe we didn't have a spark that would lead to love and a relationship like my parents, Ned's parents, and his bosses had. But we had warmth between us that I thought would make us very good friends.

And I had room for more friends.

卍 卍 卍

After the most painless breakup I'd ever had, I couldn't get my dad and Aunt Bonnie out of my mind. They'd been friends for years, but never more.

I didn't want to ask him about her in front of my mother, in case it was a sore spot—though I didn't think it was—so I went to his office a couple days later.

Dad was working on a new textbook. He found working at his office was more conducive to writing than working at the house.

His office was the equivalent of my front porch, so I understood it.

But while my front porch had a few pieces of wicker furniture, a plant, and an expansive view, my father's office was filled with a desk, an extra chair, and his books—four walls of books. His lone window was Hobbit-sized and looked at a huge pine tree, so what little natural light filtered through it had an odd green tinge to it.

I liked writing when I felt I was a part of things. My father liked writing in a literary equivalent of a solitary cave.

He looked up from his desk and smiled. "Piper, what a pleasure."

"I know I'm interrupting, but Dad, I wanted to ask you something."

He waved at the single chair that was meant for students and visitors. "Sure, honey. You know you can ask me anything."

The university had offered my father a bigger office a few times, but he'd always declined. I'd once asked him why and he said it was because he was lazy and didn't want to move all his things, but I suspected it was more than that. He liked his cave.

"It's about Aunt Bonnie," I started. "I mean, I know she was your friend, and not mom's. No, I mean, I know she was friendly with mom, but she was your friend."

I sighed. This was not coming out the way I wanted it. "I know you and Aunt Bonnie had been friends for years and she became friends with Mom because of you. I know she was a good enough friend that you made her my godmother and she took me in all those years ago. You were never specific, and I wondered if the two of you . . ."

Some people have smiley expressions. It's as if their faces' default expression is a smile.

My father's default expression was more serious. Contemplative. His natural look was one of deep thought. But when he smiled, it could light a room . . . even a cubbyhole office with weird green light.

He gave me one of those smiles now. "If you're asking what I think you're asking, then my answer is no. Bonnie and I were never together like that. We had friends who thought we would be that someday, some who even thought that we should be that, but no."

He shook his head, as if he couldn't fathom anyone thinking that. "We grew up together, you know. We built tree houses in the woods behind your grandparents' place. We rode bikes together. When Bonnie had a breakup or a fight with someone, I was her shoulder. And she . . . I don't know how to explain it other than to say that even then, I was more at home inside a book. I loved being surrounded by books. Bonnie was forever dragging me out into the world. She showed me the joy in things I'd never have noticed otherwise. She was the sister I never had. She was my best friend. She was family. Part of me has never recovered from losing her."

When Amanda was five, Aunt Bonnie got sick with the flu. Dad had talked to her and threatened to drive to Ohio that afternoon if she didn't go to her doctor.

She promised she would.

The next day he got the call from the hospital. She'd gone to the doctor's and he'd immediately had her admitted to the hospital. They'd done everything they could, but she'd died that night.

I didn't know that until later. What I remembered was Dad getting a phone call, then dropping the phone. Mom and I hurried to his side as he fell to the floor crying. Great heaving sobs.

My mother sank down next to him and simply held him as he cried out that Bonnie was dead, and Mom cried as well.

Afterward, I remember him raging, "Who dies from the flu?" almost as if he blamed Bonnie for dying. But in hindsight, maybe he simply blamed her for leaving him.

The rest of Aunt Bonnie's family had passed, so my father was her executor. I remember driving to Ohio for her funeral. A few months later, we went back to see her headstone on her grave. My father hadn't cried then, but it was almost worse. His pain rolled off him in waves.

Now, more than a decade later, I could still see that same pain. Maybe it had softened, but it was still there.

He looked at me and said, "I know that people say you can't be just a friend with someone of the opposite sex, but I think they're wrong. Bonnie was always my friend. And for a while, we thought, along with everyone else, that it might be more, but it never was."

He was lost in thought for a moment, then said, "Did I ever tell you how I met your mother?"

I shook my head. My parents loved me, but they rarely shared any intimacy of their relationship with me.

"It was Bonnie. We both went to OSU and saw each other often. One day, she met me for coffee and had a girl in tow. The girl in question was your mom. Bonnie said, *This is Tricia. I think you two need to meet, so I'm going to leave you to it.*

"That was it. She left me sitting with a total stranger at a campus coffee shop. Your mom looked as uncomfortable as I felt. She looked at me and said, 'She's . . . an original.'" She inserted this pregnant pause that made those three words seem funnier than they should have been.

"I started laughing, and then so did she. We ordered coffee and . . . Bonnie introduced me to the love of my life, and I loved Bonnie all the more for it. Does that make sense?"

I found myself nodding because it did.

"When you asked us to go away and stay with Bonnie when you had the baby, not one of us in the room doubted that Bonnie would just say yes . . . that she'd welcome you with open arms."

My question had started my father on a journey down memory lane. I sat on that couch and listened as he shared stories of my mom and Aunt Bonnie.

I know romance is the stuff that books and legends are built on, but so many of my books were built around friendship. I'd never really looked at it that way before, but as I listened to my father, the thought crystalized. Somehow, without ever really thinking about it, I'd come to believe in the power of friendship.

Friendships that were blind to gender. Friendships that were blind to age.

Friendship was as lasting as true love . . . sometimes more lasting.

My father and Aunt Bonnie had had that kind of friendship.

I'm not sure why, but I left his office feeling better.

ﷲ ﷲ ﷲ

The next day, Anthony called and told me he'd be moving to Harrisburg, the state capital, after the new year. He was going to work in the attorney general's office.

Two days before Christmas I met him for coffee across from the firm's downtown office. I'd bought him a desk plaque that read, "Anthony Long, Esquire."

"I thought about going with Anthony Long, Kick-Butt Attorney," I said, "but thought this was probably a better idea."

He'd bought me a beautifully illustrated book on urban gardens. "I thought of this gift all on my own," he assured me.

We left the coffeehouse and both went our separate ways.

I'd been wrong.

I did miss him sometimes.

Chapter Ten

Dear Amanda,

I haven't picked your journal up since I broke up with Anthony. It's not that I don't want to talk to you; it's that if—when—you get this journal, I don't want it to be full of minutia. I want to tell you the things that really matter. If I never meet you in person—if the only time we have together is that one hour—I want this to be a way to connect with you. More than that, I want it to be a way for you to feel my love.

But even though I have nothing big to say, no revelation to share, I'm bursting to the point of overflowing today. Not because of anything big. No new contract, new boyfriend . . . nothing life altering. It's mid-March here in Erie. Because the city sits on the southern edge of Lake Erie, our winters can be long, cold, and snowy. This particular winter was all those things. But today, before it's even officially spring, it's in the sixties and the snow is melting. I can see the tops of crocuses (croci?) popping through patches of dirt and snow.

The sun is out and the kids will be getting out of class soon. I'll wave to them. I have a great group of kindergarteners I read to every week, and I'm still working with Coop's class. There are some very good stories.

I guess I'm writing because I want to say that sometimes it's the very small things that matter. Ned and I walk the dogs every evening when he gets home from work. My parents are in Florida, so I haven't been going there for dinners, but most weekends I go out with Cooper or Ned.

I learned to make bread this winter.

See? Nothing big. And yet, today, sitting on my porch after a long winter, I am bursting with happiness.

I guess that's what I wanted to say . . . take time to look around your life for those small things that can mean so much.

I—

I stopped writing because Jim, my mailman, was walking toward me.

"You're out on the porch finally," he said, grinning.

"I am. It was too nice to stay inside."

He handed me a giant envelope from my publisher. I couldn't tell by the size and heft of it what was in it. I knew it wasn't books.

"Thanks," I said.

He nodded. "See you tomorrow."

"If it's as nice as this, you bet."

When he left, I sat on my chair and opened the envelope. There had to be a dozen other envelopes in it. I'd had a post office box for years, but eventually got rid of it because most of my readers contacted me online. But on occasion, some still wrote to me through my publisher.

One had a local postmark. I picked that one up first.

Dear Ms. Pip,

My mother insists that I send real thank-you notes for gifts. Not email like so many of my friends, but real letters. She says if someone goes to the trouble of getting you a gift, you can go to the trouble of writing a real letter and mailing it. And since I'm sure that you worked hard to write B Is for Bully, I thought I'd send you a real letter. So this is a thank-you note.

We have a girl in our school who is big and kind of mean. I'm not big and I don't think I'm mean. In our school, you get stuck with some definition. Jocks. Druggies. I'm a Brain. That's not how I think of myself, but I take advanced classes and I'm planning on going to college, and at my school, that makes me a brain. Winnie is a jock and she has picked on me all year. So the other day, I saw her heading toward me and I turned on the camera on my phone and hit record. She knocked me hard into my locker. All my books went flying, but I held onto my camera. She said, "Hey, genius, why don't you climb in that locker, and I'll shut the door and we'll see if you can get out?"

I picked up my phone so she was in the frame and said, "Hey, Winnie, why don't you smile for the camera?"

She went to grab it, but I said, "Go ahead; it's already gone to the cloud. You know what the cloud is, right? Since I'm a genius, I'll explain. It means that you can't get rid of it now. And I'll be posting it on YouTube and sending the link to the principal and your parents if you mess with me or anyone else in the school the rest of the year."

Anyway, she's left me alone ever since. You taught me to stand up for myself. Maybe I am a brain, but I've also got heart. And maybe now, I have some strength, too.

But your books have taught me something else, too. Kindness and forgiveness. Yesterday, Winnie was in the library working on math. I could tell she was really having trouble with it. So I walked over and said, "Just remember, whatever you do on one side of the equation, you have to do on the other." For a minute, she just looked at me and then she said, "Could you show me?"

I did.

And I thought of your book again, and wondered why she was a bully to start with. I'm meeting her tomorrow in the library to work on math again. Maybe I'll find out.

So I not only learned to save myself, but maybe I'm also learning to have empathy, too.

I read an article where you said every girl you write for is Amanda. So I'm going to say thank-you and sign this,

Amanda . . . Jo Larson

Tears were rolling down my cheeks as I finished the letter.

I didn't want to sit on my front porch and cry, so I decided to go out back and lose myself in my garden. As I rose, I knocked against my table in the process. The rest of the letters and my teacup went flying.

My favorite teacup with the forget-me-nots on it.

It hit the porch and shattered.

I didn't pause to pick up the pieces. I scooped up the letters and ran into the house, shut the door, and dumped the letters on the table. I didn't stop. I walked through the house to the back door and into the garden. I made my way back to Ned's bench, still crying.

It felt like Amanda, my Amanda, had sent the letter and approved of what I tried to do in my stories.

I know it didn't make sense. I'd heard from readers in the past, but this one touched me even before I got to her signature.

My emotions were a jumble.

I'm not sure how long I sat there, but suddenly Ned was at the gate, calling my name. "Pip. Pip."

"I'm back here," I called. I straightened out the slightly crumpled letter.

He thundered through the garden, straight back to the bench. "I knocked on the front door and you didn't answer. I was scared to death when you didn't answer. What the hell happened?"

"Nothing. I'm fine." I knew even as I said the words, trying to claim I was fine was ridiculous. I was an ugly crier.

Coop once came over to cry on my shoulder after a breakup. And I mean that literally. She looked just as pretty crying as she normally did.

Actually, maybe even better.

There was a certain vulnerability in her tears that was missing from her regular life.

I didn't look pretty or vulnerable. I looked snotty and bloated.

"Really, despite how I look, I'm fine," I said.

Ned didn't say anything. He held my broken teacup in his hand and quirked his eyebrow.

I knew he was waiting for a better explanation. "I got a letter from a reader that struck a chord."

"Not a good chord," he said and without my asking, he sat down next to me and wrapped his arms around me.

"I'm not sure what she said, and I'm not asking." He hugged me. It was something my mom might have done if she found me crying, but there was nothing parental in Ned's embrace.

And there was nothing sexual either.

His hug had friendship and empathy wrapped in it.

I could have called Cooper or my mom. Even my dad. But I was glad it was Ned who'd found me.

I thought of my dad and Aunt Bonnie and knew that Ned was family to me, the same way Aunt Bonnie had been for my dad.

"Thanks," I said, my voice muffled against his chest.

His words rumbled as he said, "You're welcome."

Later that night, I went back to the journal.

And picked up where I left off.

—I got a letter today as I was writing to you. It was from a reader. Her story touched me. She said my book had touched her.

There is a chest that's full of letters like that waiting for you to read someday. I've answered them all. But this one letter I'm enclosing in your notebook. I've said for years that every girl I write for, every girl that Amanda's Pantry feeds, or Amanda's Closet gives a coat to, is you. And part of me always believed that. But this one letter, I felt it to the core of my being.

I'll be writing Jo back. And while I've always written fiction, I'm thinking about writing some nonfiction, and I think I want to start with Jo's story.

Love,
Piper

Chapter Eleven

It was April again.

As I get older, I notice that time seems to accelerate. Days slip into weeks, into months, into years . . .

I wonder if time moves slower for Amanda than it does for me?

There'd been an article in the paper about Anthony a few days ago. In the interview he was asked if he was dating. He said he'd met someone in Harrisburg.

I was happy that he was moving on. Truly, I wanted only the best for him.

But I wanted the best for me, too. I simply didn't know what that was.

I ran my hand through the scruff on Bruce's neck. He was the only physical contact I had with another being for whole days at a time. And as much as I loved my dog, I was coming to realize I wanted more.

I sat in my backyard on what I'd come to think of as Ned's bench and tried to envision what my *more* would look like.

I didn't know. My life was full of writing and volunteering. I loved what I did. I don't think my *more* had anything to do with another thing.

Maybe I needed to date? Maybe there was someone out there for me.

I thought about Anthony. He had no trouble moving on. I don't think I would have trouble either if I had a vision of what I was moving toward.

The small bell I'd found at a house sale and put on my garden gate rang. Soon, Ned came into sight around the springtime greenery. "Why are you sitting back here?"

"Because it's not raining." That truly summed up my reasoning.

It had been such a wet spring. My tulips and daffodils were now being joined by leaves and buds on the trees and bushes. My service-berries were covered in white blossoms. Yes, *not raining* really was all it took to drive me into the yard. I didn't mention that heavy thoughts had also brought me here.

Some people might have wondered about my reasoning, but Ned didn't question it. "Trouble with the new book?" When I didn't say anything immediately, he added, "I know this is where you like to think."

"I am thinking," I admitted. I thought about letting that explanation suffice, but Ned was a friend who deserved better. I softly added, "I'm thinking that there's a chance that I'm broken."

He didn't try to reassure me that wasn't the case. He simply asked, "In what way?"

Maybe when I gave away my daughter I gave away too much of my heart to have anything left over to share with anyone else. I almost said those words.

But I couldn't manage it. It was as if I'd given Amanda to her parents, but selfishly held onto the thoughts of her because I was unwilling to share anything else.

Yes, maybe I was broken. "Maybe some fundamental piece of me is missing. Look how I treated Anthony."

Ned snorted. "Yeah, you were just awful to him." His voice dripped with a sarcastic lilt. "Yes, awful. You found out the two of you wanted very different things and so you ended things with kindness. You kept him as a friend. Yes, Pip, you're an ogre. Is this about that interview where he said he was seeing someone?"

I shook my head and answered honestly, "No. Not really. Not in an I-regret-letting-him-go way, but I'm questioning . . . well, everything."

Ned didn't say anything.

"Do you know what I felt when I heard the man I was with for a year was moving to Harrisburg to work at a job I suspect he'd dreamed of? Not happiness for him, and not even worry that I'd miss him. I felt relief. Relief that I wasn't feeling like I had to go with him. And today, when I read he was dating, I felt even more relief that I could let go of some of that guilt as well."

"So if you're so relieved, why are you back here brooding?" Ned asked.

Brooding? Maybe. "Frankly, there's no earthly reason I couldn't have moved to some other city. My work is very portable, and there are hungry people everywhere. There are children who read my books everywhere. So do you know why I was so relieved? Because I am self-ish. I didn't want to move. It was all about me. A relationship has to be about both people. About what they both want. About being willing to compromise. I am obviously too selfish for a real relationship."

There—I'd said the words.

I added, "I'm glad Anthony's found someone who's not as selfish as me."

Ned didn't try to tell me I wasn't selfish. Instead he segued in an entirely different direction. "I've read all your books, you know."

That wasn't what I'd expected to hear. "Pardon?"

He nodded. "All of them. I bought every one of them. I stacked them in order of publication and read them all back-to-back over the course of a couple months. And I figured out a few things about you."

I'd always felt that the best fiction books were semi-autobiograph-ical. Especially YAs. I might have grown up decades before my readers, but there's a universality in childhood. And it's there in the teen years, too—the heartache, the sense of discovery, the sense of isolation and being misunderstood. The worries about the future.

I knew there were pieces of me in each book—Mom and Coop caught them sometimes. I thought of them like movie Easter eggs. Even though I knew they were there, I wasn't sure that others could find them. "What do you think you know about me?"

"You have innate kindness. I knew that, but your books really drove the point home. It's there in every character, on every page. And you have a sense of justice."

I didn't respond because frankly, I didn't know what to say.

After a pregnant pause, Ned said, "And when you love, you love with your whole heart.

"That last part is why I am positive you never loved Anthony. You liked him. You cared for him. You might have enjoyed his company, but Pip, when you finally fall in love, you'd do anything for that person. You'd give up anything, go anywhere for him. You did not love Anthony, so letting him go was a kindness. It wasn't selfishness."

"I don't know." I thought there was a chance I'd love Anthony, despite the fact I'd never felt a spark or fell head over heels. I thought that maybe an adult love didn't require that rush of emotion.

He snorted. "Trust me, I know. You don't have a selfish bone in your body."

I knew he was wrong about that, but I didn't argue the point. Instead, I asked, "You read them all? All my books?"

"Every single one. I also have a collection of some of the articles you wrote early on. Including a certain article on the history of sofas. I think Chesterfields are a fine variety."

I laughed along with Ned, which I knew had been his intention. But my laughter turned to tears. Ned opened up his arms and held me.

It felt like coming home.

When I stopped crying, I reluctantly pulled back. "Sorry," I said as I brushed at the damp spot on his shoulder.

"No problem. I actually came over to see if you wanted to go for a walk," Bruce, who'd followed me out back, popped up at the word. "I know that it's earlier than most days, but I have a case I need to work on tonight."

"Would Princess like a sleepover?" It had become our routine for Princess to sleep over on nights Ned worked late. I never asked for specifics on cases, but I knew occasionally he liked to track down difficult-to-reach people at night.

"I'm pretty sure Princess would love it."

I went into the house with Bruce at my heels. When I reached for his lead, his happiness knew no bounds.

Maybe I needed to stop brooding. Anthony was happy. And me? I looked at my goofy dog, trying to catch his own tail, as if he was worried it wouldn't get to go for a walk otherwise.

I realized I was happy, too.

I couldn't second-guess what was on my horizon.

I was simply going to accept what came my way with a sense of joy.

We'd fallen into a walking rhythm. I walked on the left, Ned on the right, and the two dogs were in front of us, echoing our positions. We walked through the school playground and then three blocks over, ten blocks up, another three blocks over and then back. We'd clocked it and it was about two miles.

As someone who spent the great part of her day sitting, I was becoming very aware of staying fit. I was in my thirties,

The thirties sounded so old to me when I was in my twenties; now, they didn't seem too bad, but I knew my forties were just a blink away, so I walked and tried to stay fit.

Ned and I didn't talk much. We simply let the dogs do their thing.

We waved at neighbors. We'd walked this route so often there were a bunch we knew by sight, and some we knew by name.

Tony and Julie were out at their house. His name made me think of Anthony, but before I could start brooding again, I cut the thought off.

Tony had a flat of garden plants and the three of us happily chatted about our gardens.

"I'm starting to feel like the odd man out," Ned complained. The only garden he had was the small bed of flowers out front that I'd convinced him to let me put in last year.

"Don't listen to him," I told Tony and Julie. "I took him over some tomatoes last year and he smugly assured me he didn't need to have a garden as long as he had me."

The sentence came out a bit awkwardly, as if we were more than we were.

". . . next door," I added, which actually made it worse, I realized.

Julie laughed and said, "I'd make him pull some weeds this season. Make him earn his produce."

"I might," I said. "We'd better head back. Ned's got an appointment."

I purposefully didn't say anything, hoping Ned hadn't noticed my awkward moment.

When we got back to our places, he said, "Let me go get ready and I'll bring Princess over."

"Sounds good."

Fifteen minutes later, he was at my door with a box and the dog.

"I got you something," he said as he thrust the box at me and unclipped Princess, who ran to find Bruce.

"For what?" I asked.

"Just open it and you'll see."

I opened the cardboard box and found . . . my teacup. The one I broke. Well, not actually mine, but the same kind.

He grinned. "I stuck the base in my pocket. It had the pattern's name and its maker on it. I found it on a china replacement site. You can get a whole set of this if you like it that much."

"How did you know I liked it that much?" I asked, fingering the fine bone china. It was an exact replica of the one I'd broken.

"I know you've got a bunch of teacups, but this is your go-to one. You were upset when you broke it."

I didn't know what to say.

It turned out I didn't have to say anything because Ned wasn't done surprising me.

"I wondered if you want to go out to a movie and dinner this weekend."

I loved going to the movies with Ned. He never said anything during the film, but afterward I could count on a rousing discussion. "Sure. Did I miss a new sci-fi one?"

"No, not our regular science fiction friends sort of movie." He looked at me and said, "A date."

There are certain things that never cross a person's mind. How many news reports include a friend of the perpetrator who exclaims, *I had no idea he/she* . . . whatever they'd done.

If Ned had said he was a fugitive I don't think I'd have been more surprised than I was when he said the word *date*. I repeated it just to be sure I'd heard correctly. "A date? With you?"

"Don't sound so shocked." He looked more amused than insulted.

"I mean, a date? Us?" When I wrote, I could place characters neatly into their boxes. Protagonist, antagonist. Hero, heroine. Best friend. Boy next door. Classmate. Enemy. Frenemy. Yes, there was overlap, but most characters had a firm description in my head.

Ned was in the *best friend* box, right up there with Cooper.

To be honest, probably closer to me than Coop, who had a new boyfriend and she'd been preoccupied with him the last few months.

What if we dated and it didn't work? I'd lose Ned as a friend.

No, that was a stupid cop-out. I'd broken up with Anthony, and we'd stayed friends. I mean, if I got arrested, he's the attorney I'd call.

I'd broken up with Anthony because I wasn't in love with him. I was in like with him. Very much in like.

I was in like with Ned as well. I had been since he moved in. And for half a moment when I met him, there had been a spark, but I'd snuffed it out the moment I found out he had a girlfriend. Could a spark be rekindled, and more . . . could it grow into something deeper after all this time?

"I can see you thinking," Ned said. "You're running through a bunch of scenarios. What if we dated and it didn't work out? Could we still be friends? What if we dated and it did work out? What then? What if . . ."

"Yes," I admitted. "I don't want to lose you."

"Here's something else I know from our walks and talks, and from reading your books . . . running through multiple scenarios is a big part of your profession. But maybe just this once, you don't. Maybe you simply try a date with me and see how it goes."

"What if I lose you in the process?" I asked. That was my true fear. I'd come to count on Ned in a way I didn't count on anyone else. Not even Coop.

He pulled me close. I thought he might kiss me, but he didn't. He simply held me and said, "Of all the scenarios that you can imagine, take that one off the table. You're my friend. My best friend, truth be told. I think there could be more between us, but I'm absolutely certain there can't be less."

I'd thought something similar about Anthony. He was a friend. I will never know how I could have thought he was anything more than that, but I knew for a fact he'd never be anything less.

If I could know that about Anthony, how could I doubt that, no matter what, I'd always have a firm friendship with Ned? Like Dad and Aunt Bonnie.

"Pip, if we try it and it doesn't work out, we'll go back to being us and someday laugh about the failed attempt," he promised.

"But . . ."

Ned put a finger to my lips. "Just say yes."

I was still nervous, but I realized that I wanted to know the answer to this particular what-if. What if we did date and it worked out?

I took a deep breath and said, "Yes."

"Great. I'll put a date together. Saturday?"

I nodded. "So if you're planning it, what you're saying is, I have to wear something better than this?" I lifted up a knee, where a new hole was forming.

"You can wear whatever you want, but this is a real dinner at a sit-down restaurant, not pizza in your jungle."

I nodded. "Yeah, that's a grown-up clothes sort of evening then."

I did the only thing a woman in my position could do.

I called Coop.

Big mistake.

On Saturday, I found myself at the mall with her as she said the words, "Now, let's shop for makeup."

We'd already shopped for clothes and shoes. She'd even made me buy a new purse. I wasn't sure I could handle shopping for makeup, too. "Really, there's no need. I have makeup. Why on earth would I need more?"

"When's the last time you used makeup?" she asked.

I had to think about it. "The Amanda's Pantry dinner last year."

"Yeah, just toss that all out. We're starting from scratch."

"Coop, seriously—"

"I have never heard anyone whine so much about shopping."

"I really, really hate shopping."

"Really?" Coop asked, sarcasm dripping from her voice. "Because I couldn't tell."

I hefted the bags I was carrying. "I could have bought all this online."

Coop shook her head and looked stubborn. I noticed as we walked we were moving toward the makeup counter.

"No," she said firmly. "You couldn't have shopped for this online, because if you did, you'd have bought the dress you tried on first. It was a size too big. So rather than look sexy, you'd have looked frumpy."

"Ned's used to me looking like this. He wouldn't have minded the larger, more comfortable dress."

"I'm sure he wouldn't have minded, but he wouldn't have been blown away by it. This one, he'll be blown away by." She smiled, as if she was the one personally responsible for my impressing Ned.

"I don't necessarily want to blow him away. And let's be honest, he knows what I generally look like. He knows I won't maintain this look for any length of time."

"One look at you in this and he'll forget everything he's ever known."

"Coop—" I started to protest.

She cut me off. "Listen, you two have danced around this since he first moved in. When it's just you and me together, do you have any idea how often you say his name? *Ned said this. Ned did that.* Or *Ned and I* . . . You two have been an item for years; you simply didn't realize it. Everyone else did. Mela did. And I'm pretty sure Anthony did. I did. And I bet if you called your parents, they did."

"If you all thought that I . . . that we . . . Why didn't anyone say anything?"

"Because it wouldn't have mattered. Not until you were ready. I've known Mark since high school. But it wasn't until this year, when he started teaching with me, that I realized there was more than just friendship."

Coop hadn't said much about Mark, but every time she did mention him, she practically glowed. "I'd like a chance to see you two together."

"Maybe you, me, Mark, and Ned can go out sometime," Coop said.

Talking about going out with Ned as a couple was odd. There was a difference between me and Ned doing something, and me-and-Ned-the-couple doing something.

I asked the question that was haunting me. "What if Ned and I try it out and it doesn't work? What if we mess up our friendship in the process?" Ned had reassured me, but I wanted to hear Coop say the words, too.

Rather than reassurances, she scolded me. "You can't live your whole life afraid of making a mistake, worrying about what might happen."

"What if . . . ?" I said more to myself than to Coop, but she heard me.

"Right. Those kinds of worrying questions can paralyze you. Go out and knock his socks off. Let what comes next find its own way."

I nodded. I was going to try.

⚘ ⚘ ⚘

I finished dressing and looked in the mirror. I was pretty sure with Coop's help I'd gotten beyond my normal six or seven. I thought I might actually be dressed to the eights.

I jumped at the sound of the doorbell. I looked at the clock. Ned was early. I ran down the stairs to the front door. My palms were sweating as I opened it.

But it wasn't Ned. "Mom?"

"Wow," was all she said. "Where are you going?" She stepped inside.

I shut the door. "Just dinner," I said, though I knew there was no *just* about it. Tonight could change everything. I wasn't sure I wanted anything to change.

I liked my life. There was a rhythm to it.

I liked my friendship with Ned. I could count on it.

"I don't think any woman in the history of the world has gone out to *just dinner* dressed like that," she said.

"Is something wrong?" I tugged at my hem. I'd thought it was a bit too short, but Coop had assured me it was just right.

"No, nothing's wrong. You look lovely. So who's the guy?" she asked as she came into the house.

"Ned," I admitted.

"Finally." She packed a lot into that one word.

"What do you mean, *finally*?" I asked, although I was pretty sure she was going to join in the Coop serenade.

"Honey, your dad and I have always wondered why you and Ned weren't dating. It's as obvious as the nose on my face that there's something between you."

"We're friends," I said.

If dating didn't work, we'd still be friends. I kept reminding myself that Anthony and I had stayed friends, so there was no reason that Ned and I couldn't manage it, but still . . .

"Your dad and I are friends, too. Some people are destined for simple friendship, but for some, that friendship is the basis for something more. You can be friends with someone you love. Honestly, I think the best romantic relationships have a deep friendship at their core."

I thought of Aunt Bonnie. She and my dad had never been more than friends. But with my mom . . .

Mom continued, "Yes, you and Ned are friends, but I think, if you let it, there's more between you two."

I said, "We're going to see if there is."

"Good. I just stopped by to see if you wanted to come over for pizza tonight." She laughed. "I think your plans are probably going to be better."

"I hope so," I said, more to myself than her. To be honest, I wished Ned had asked me for pizza. That would have been easy. I know how to do pizza with Ned. I looked down at my outfit. I wasn't sure I knew how to do this with him.

"Enjoy yourself, honey," Mom said.

"I'd enjoy myself more if I weren't all dressed up," I muttered.

"You're going to knock Ned's socks off."

"I kind of like his socks exactly where there are," I said. I liked things the way they were. I shouldn't have said yes to this date.

"Have fun," my mother said.

I walked her to the door and opened it to see Ned. He was dressed beyond the eights and was definitely in the nine-ish zone. I thought the word *wow*, but didn't say it out loud.

I just drank in the sight of him. He was my Ned, but more.

He didn't say anything either.

We just stood there, looking at each other, and I'll confess, I forgot my mom was there until she said, "Well, you two obviously don't need me here," and left.

As she left, I realized Ned had Princess with him. "Princess wanted to spend the evening with Bruce, if that's okay," he said.

"That's fine."

He unclipped her and let her into the house. Princess disappeared inside, looking for Bruce.

Ned extended his arm. "Shall we?"

I put my arm in his and we left.

I had high hopes for our date.

In the end, my hopes were the highest point of the date.

Dear Amanda,

It's been a week since my date with Ned. I've wondered why it was such a flop. It was as if we couldn't find anything to talk about and while Ned looked great and I looked as good as I could, it was as if the clothes just served to remind us both that this was more than one of the countless meals we'd shared. Meals where we never ran out of things to talk about.

I was so thankful when we got to the movies, but even that was different too. It was a Saturday night, and I don't think either of us had given any thought to the fact that Saturdays are date nights. The theater was packed with couples.

The show we wanted to see was sold out, so we took the only other one that started in the same time slot. It was a morbid story of obsessive love that ended with one character dead and the other in jail. Not my kind of movie. Ned's either, to be honest.

We pulled into Ned's driveway and he went to change before coming over to get Princess. I changed as well.

When he came back, we were just Ned and Pip again. And that made all the difference.

I'm not saying that dressing up and going out on the town doesn't have its place, but I'm saying that maybe the best relationships don't need makeup and high heels. Maybe they just need someone who likes you just the way you are.

Love,
Piper

I didn't go into detail about it in the journal, but Ned came back over after the date wearing a T-shirt and jeans. I'd torn out of my dress and put on yoga pants and a *B Is for Bully* T-shirt.

He came in, took one look at me, and said, "There you are."

"And there you are, too."

And without waiting for an invitation, I walked into his arms. And what started out as an end-of-date, goodnight kiss, became an introduction.

Ned didn't go home that night.

The next morning, we took Princess and Bruce for a walk, all four of us in our normal formation, until Ned reached over and took my hand.

It was a new configuration to our walk.

We've been walking that way ever since.

Senior Year

Chapter Twelve

I sat on my porch for another first day of school. It would be Amanda's last first day of high school. She was on the cusp of adulthood.

The thought brought a mix of emotions and I wondered what she was planning to do when she graduated. Move on to a university somewhere? A year abroad? Straight into the workforce?

She was on my mind as I watched the annual chaos across the street. Last year's students were all moving up a grade, and transfer students were joining them on the front lawn of the school, waiting for the bell to ring and start not just another school day but another school year.

Cooper had come over for an early breakfast. She'd been back at school a couple of weeks, getting ready for her students. But today was special, so I made her waffles and she bubbled over about her plans for the year. She warned me that the students had loved last year's books, so this year's class would expect to do them, which meant I should plan on some visits.

I was thrilled at the chance. I loved Coop's enthusiasm for what she does.

Before she left, I'd handed her a bagged lunch with "Miss Cooper" printed boldly on the side.

She'd laughed and carried it off as she crossed the street.

Kids walked by and called out their hi-Miss-Pips. The littler ones chased each other and shrieked, while the older kids stood in clusters and tried to look cool.

I enjoyed the show. I had a cup of tea in my very proper forget-me-not teacup. The original had always been my favorite, but this replica was doubly so. Every time I used it, I thought of Ned. Those thoughts warmed me more than the tea.

I tried to work but couldn't seem to manage it. The hustle and bustle across the street was a distraction. I finally gave up pretending to work.

I closed my eyes and let myself really listen to the sounds. A squeak of the metal teeter-totter. Cars rolling past. Car doors opening and slamming shut. A horn. And beneath all of that, the buzz of the children's voices. Shouting greetings. Talking loudly. Laughing.

The word *cacophony* came to mind.

This was a wonderful example of a joyous cacophony.

The bell rang and I opened my eyes. A number of kids bolted toward the front doors. Others followed at an even pace. And a few walked so slowly they were almost moving backward.

Eventually they all disappeared into the school. Another bell rang and I knew they were heading into their new classrooms. They were meeting their new teachers, getting new books.

They were happy, afraid, excited.

Maybe I liked writing for kids because they had a life of endless possibilities in front of them. Whether they were living an idyllic childhood or a troubled one, they could become anything they wanted to be.

It was warm. More than warm, it was downright hot. I had on a pair of capris and a tank top. My hair was pulled into a high ponytail, so it didn't touch my neck. It had been a cool summer, so to have such a hot day for the first day of school seemed slightly unfair.

It always seemed that cooler first days of school set the proper atmosphere.

I sat there thinking about the weather rather than writing. I finally admitted that I was not going to get any work done on my book, so I gave up. I went inside and got the journal, which is what I'd wanted all along.

I hadn't written in it much this summer. It wasn't that Amanda wasn't on my mind or even that I was running out of things I wanted to say to her. It was that the blank pages in the journal were dwindling, and I was becoming very discriminating about what I wrote now. I wanted these last pages to count.

But even though I had nothing earth-shattering to share this morning, I still wanted to write something. It was her first day of her senior year of high school.

Oh, I knew I could be off. She had one of those birthdays on the cusp of school rules. Maybe her parents held her back an extra year and she wouldn't graduate until next year, or maybe she was a prodigy and had started school early. Heck, if she was an academic prodigy, she could be in college already. But after consulting about summer birthdays with Coop under the guise of using it for a book—which I did, so that wasn't a lie—I was pretty sure I was correct and this was her final year of high school.

The schoolyard was quiet now, except for an occasional straggler. I picked up the journal.

Dear Amanda,
It's the first day of school here and my thoughts are on you. You'll be a senior this year.

What if you were here and we were talking in person? What sort of advice would I give you?

I guess I'd have to say my biggest advice would be, don't be in a hurry for this year to pass. It will do that in its own time. So enjoy the moments. Enjoy your classes and your classmates. Enjoy the sense of possibility in all the things that will follow high school. The world is your oyster. I'm not sure why that's a saying, but it is.

Enjoy this last year of being your parents' child. When you leave for college, that will change. Oh, you'll always be their daughter, but you'll be meeting them as one adult to another.

I know the dynamics of my relationship with my parents changed when I left for OSU.

To be honest, it shifted when I was pregnant. My parents allowed me to decide what to do. They supported me the whole way. And after that, they treated me as an adult. It colored my last years of school.

I hope your year is a happy one and that you savor all the moments and milestones.

Know that you're in my thoughts, as always.

Love,
Piper

"You've got the book out," Ned said.

I jumped, startled. "I'm going to have to bell you like a cat. You're too quiet."

"Ah, so it's a bear-trap day, huh?" He grinned and leaned against the porch railing.

I closed the journal and walked to the edge of the porch, leaned over, and kissed him. It shouldn't have seemed novel after all these months, but it did. Novel and wonderful . . . and right.

Every time I was in his arms I wondered why it had taken so long.

I kissed him again just because I could. "Not a bear trap at all."

He walked around the porch and up the stairs. "I don't have to be to work for another hour." It was a statement, but it was laced with suggestion and an invitation.

"Turns out, it's the first day of school and I can't work, so I've decided to play hooky. The only problem is, I don't know what to do with myself if I'm not working."

"I have a suggestion or two," Ned offered as he led me toward the door. I grabbed the journal and followed him inside, anxious to hear just what he was suggesting.

Maybe I'd make a few suggestions of my own.

⚘ ⚘ ⚘

Ned and I fell into a new routine as our relationship moved from spring to summer and finally into fall. We walked the dogs. He came with me to weekend meals and picnics at my folks'. And he spent the night at my house more often than at his own.

When he traveled, Princess came to stay with me.

I'd been in other relationships and worried about where they were going or what would happen next, but with Ned, it was as if the friendship that we'd shared for years accommodated the new dimension in our relationship without straining.

I took his advice and didn't allow myself to ask what if. I lived in the moment and I didn't worry or try to see into the future.

As the holidays approached, I realized I couldn't imagine my life without Ned any more. He'd become part of not just the new rhythm of my life, but part of me.

He'd eased his way into every aspect. My mornings now started with him. In the warmer weather, we took our coffee and papers out into the backyard and sat in companionable silence as we passed sections back and forth.

As the weather cooled, we sat at the kitchen table, watching my backyard's wild landscape shift and alter. Leaves fell, flowers died back, birds came more frequently to the feeders.

When fall gave way to winter and it started to snow, our relationship showed no signs of ebbing. Ned and I started our days with snow shovels in hand. Occasionally shovels gave way to snowballs. Mrs. W. came out after one particularly rambunctious fight and rather than scold us about the racket we were making, she threw two snowballs of her own . . . and hit us both.

Turned out, Mrs. W. had a good arm for an eighty-something-year-old.

Then she invited us in for hot chocolate and thanked us for the umpteenth time for taking care of her sidewalk and drive.

I told her that's what neighbors do.

She assured me that not all of them do and I thought that was a shame.

Christmas arrived early, though I ignored the too-early decorations and waited to begin my personal celebration until after Thanksgiving.

I'd always adored the season. It was as if for a short span of weeks every year, people remembered to be kind to one another. Donations came in at Amanda's Pantry. People asked to volunteer.

People smiled, despite the record snowfalls.

Christmas music played nonstop on the radio.

I love Christmas, but this year more than most. I knew the difference was Ned.

I'd spent Christmases with him before, but this was the first time we were together. It was the first Christmas that he was my *boyfriend*.

I used the word for lack of a better one, but it felt way too high-school-ish, and really didn't do justice to how I felt about Ned.

Not that either of us had put our feelings into words.

I didn't feel rushed or pressured. I was sure of my feelings and felt confident in his for me. Whatever this stage of our relationship was called, it was good.

The only fly in my ointment was what to get him for Christmas.

I went round and round about what to buy him.

I went shopping with Cooper and with Mom. I found a lot of things I thought he'd like. I bought an antique toy detective kit at one of Mom's favorite antique stores. I bought him a sweater and a new series of mystery novels. He wasn't much of a reader, but I couldn't imagine buying someone gifts that didn't include a book or two.

Still, I looked for that one special present.

And then it hit me.

I laughed with relief, and wondered why it took me so long to find the present. It was simple and perfect.

On Christmas morning, I woke up first, grabbed my ratty black cable-knit sweater that I wore instead of a bathrobe and tiptoed out of the room.

A few years ago, my mom had bought me some buffalo plaid flannel pajama pants. I'd worn them for the holiday and caught sight of them when I plugged in the tree. They were starting to wear a bit thin but were still my favorite pajama pants.

Both dogs followed me down. While they were outside, I started coffee and turned on my iPod Christmas playlist.

Steve and Eydie were soon crooning about having a merry Christmas.

Ned walked into the kitchen, pulled me into his arms and sang along as he twirled me around. I laughed, not because it was funny, but because at that moment, I had so much utter joy inside me that it had to go somewhere. A laugh seemed just the thing.

"Merry Christmas," I said, my head still pressed against his bare chest. Ned wore boxers and padded around the house barefoot while I wore heavy socks and slippers. He never seemed to get cold.

It worked out well for me because he never complained when I stole the covers.

The dogs barked and I reluctantly left his arms to let them in. I handed him a cup of coffee. "That definitely makes it merrier," he assured me.

After we fed the dogs, we went out to the tree.

"Can I go first?" I asked.

He nodded. I hurried to the small pile of gifts I'd bought him and pulled the smallest box off the top of the pile. "I went round and round about what to buy you." I handed it to him.

Ned was not a neat paper puller. He tore through the pretty wrapping and tossed it on the floor. Princess pounced on it, assuming he'd meant it for her, and Bruce opened one eye, then shut it after deciding paper wasn't something worth waking up for.

Ned opened the box. He pulled out the key on the Star Trek Enterprise key ring. The key ring was an extra little bit of fun for the gift.

Ned looked at me with questions in his eyes.

"It's a key to my house," I explained.

"Pip, I already have a key to your house," he said, obviously still confused. "I've had it since shortly after I moved in next door."

"No, you have *myyyyy*," I dragged out and put a heavy emphasis on the word *my*, "emergency set of keys that I store at your house. This is *your* key to my house. What I'm saying is you can come and go as you please . . . and I hope you please often."

Understanding dawned in his eyes. He leaned forward and kissed me. I kissed him back.

I'd never given Anthony a key.

As my lips pressed to Ned's, I wondered how I could have ever believed I loved anyone else.

Love.

Neither of us had said the word, but I was pretty sure that's what this feeling was.

I'd complained about not feeling a spark with Anthony but realized as I watched Ned open his gifts, I'd felt it for Ned, and, when I allowed it to burn, it had settled into a warm glow.

It was no raging fire. I didn't meet him and instantly know that this was the man I was destined to spend my life with. I'd gotten over my initial worry about taking our relationship beyond friendship. I knew that no matter what, Ned would be in my life. Since I settled that, I'd had no questions or qualms about us as a couple.

Instead, falling in love with Ned had been so easy, it had happened without any fuss or fanfare. That didn't make the love less. In fact, I thought it made for a stronger, more stable love.

I'd never been the one to tell someone I loved him easily, and never first, but I had no fear or anxiety about saying the words to Ned. As our kiss slowed, I said, "I love you, you know."

He nodded and grinned. "Of course you do. I mean what's not to love?" We both laughed and he pulled me close. "I love you, too, you know."

"I do," I admitted. "But you only love me *two*. I love you *one*."

He caught my play on the word *too* and rolled his eyes. "Goof."

He gave me a teapot that matched the teacup he'd replaced. It was a lovely, thoughtful gift. But the best gift I received for Christmas was Ned's love.

Dear Amanda,

It's Christmas again. I'm sitting by the front window, waiting for Ned to get done clearing snow. Erie took the term white Christmas to heart this year. We both cleared our sidewalks and Mrs. W.'s, but a car got stuck in a drive down the block and he went to help.

I've spent holidays with Ned before, but this was our first Christmas together as a couple. I told him I loved him.

Sometimes in books people agonize over saying those words, or hearing them, but with Ned, it was natural. Easy, even. I could give him that piece of my heart and know that he'd protect it.

I added another charm to your bracelet this year. A graduation cap. I know you've got a few months to go, and at your age, that feels like forever, but it's the blink of an eye.

I suspect that the end of May will be busy for you. It will be poignant for me. You'll be in my thoughts.

I wonder what your plans are after you graduate. College? A job?

I hope whatever path you take, you're happy.

As someone who's living in the glow of a new love, I can tell you that happy matters.

The pages in this journal are almost full. When I finish them all, I'll tuck it up in Talia Piper Eliason's antique wedding chest . . . your chest. It will be there, along with the letters from Amanda's Pantry, all the books I wrote for you, and your bracelet.

When this journal is full and I've told your story here, I need you to know that you'll still always be on my mind.

More than that, you'll always be in my heart.

It's just now, instead of you being there alone, Ned is there as well.

Merry Christmas.

All My Love,
Piper

Chapter Thirteen

"Deep breath, Pip," Ned commanded as he stood next to my dad at the bottom of my staircase.

I needed the reminder. I'd been bubbling over with excitement all day.

March was one of those in-between months. Not quite winter, not quite spring.

In between. That's how I'd felt all day. Not quite excited, not quite nervous. I swung between the two emotions like a pendulum, neither one thing nor the other for long. Ned was right; breathing seemed to be something optional.

I took a second and forced myself to inhale. I exhaled as I stepped off the last step.

Coop and my mom followed me down the stairs.

I told myself to capture this moment so that I could savor it once it passed. I was surrounded by the people I loved and about to go to an event that celebrated a project I was passionate about. It was a moment that deserved to be preserved.

My mother moved next to my father, as if they were drawn to one another by some invisible force. Coop and Ned took up positions on either side of me. Friends I couldn't do without—friends I knew I'd never *have* to do without.

The dogs even seemed to sense my bubbling emotions. They danced around at the foot of the steps, pulling me from my moment.

"Down," I warned them. Even they went into my save-the-moment snapshot.

"If your beasts mess up that dress . . . well, no dog bones for a month," Coop threated them.

"Week," she corrected, then sighed as Bruce and Princess realized she was talking to them and sat down in front of her.

Coop leaned down and petted them both. "Fine. You'd still get bones, but I'd be very disappointed in you."

"Sucker," Ned said to Coop, then turned to me. "How does she handle a class of eighth graders?"

"I'm very scary," Coop said at the same time I said, "They love her, so they listen."

My version was more truthful than hers.

I glanced at the clock, wanting to be sure I'd be on time.

Ned noticed and said, "You've got plenty of time."

"You've done a lot of talks before, honey," Mom said. "And I don't think I've ever seen you so worked up."

"This is different, Mom. This isn't about me or my books. It's about the kids who worked so hard on these stories. It's about the stories they shared. I'm so thrilled to be a part of the project."

After that letter from Jo Larson, I went to the school board with Coop at my side. She'd helped me teacher-up my proposal. With her help and the school board's backing, we'd put together a book of stories written by school district students.

I always get excited when a new release arrives at my door, but this time *excited* seemed an inadequate description. I trembled the first time I held a copy of *Raise Your Hands: Stories from Today's Classrooms.*

Not only had Jo and other school district students contributed to it, the cover art was done by an amazing student artist. One of the English classes had proofed the book and one of the computer classes formatted it.

The district was charging for both print and e-book versions, and all the funds were going to support the libraries.

My school—well, technically, not *my* school, but the school across the street—had agreed to host the *release* party. I was going to speak and introduce the project. Afterward, there was a book signing. All the students who'd participated were invited to take part.

I walked across the street with my small entourage.

"I'm going to go try to corral the beasts," Coop said. "Because I'm so tough," she added.

I wasn't sure if she was trying to remind us or herself. But if reminding us was her goal, I'm pretty sure the chorus of laughter that followed her told her we weren't buying her *toughness*.

"I'm going to get a seat," Dad said as he kissed my cheek outside the auditorium door. "I need you to know how very, very proud we are of you, Piper. You've always made us very proud."

I felt myself begin to tear up, but Mom scolded him, "Don't you dare make her cry."

Dad grinned and hurried into the auditorium.

Mom turned to me. "And don't listen to your dad and tear up. You'll mess up your makeup." Then she leaned forward and kissed my cheek. "But he's right; we are proud."

Hey, Miss Pips rang out as we walked to the stage entrance. Mom headed toward the opposite wing and Ned held my hand and waited on our side of the stage. "I don't want to risk your mother's wrath and make you tear up again, but for what it's worth, I'm proud of you, too. And I want to talk to you about something later."

"What?" Vague comments like that were not normally Ned's MO.

"I was thinking . . . that maybe it's time to think about selling my place. I—"

He was nervous, I realized. Whether he was nervous I would say no, or simply nervous about the suggestion, I wasn't sure, but I was absolutely positive about my answer.

I interrupted him. "Yes. You haven't spent a night at your place since before Christmas. You live with me in all but name. I think it's a great idea."

"Well, that's part of it. But more than selling my place . . ." He took a deep breath. "I was thinking we should get married," he blurted out in a very uncharacteristic way. "I know, I'm doing this all wrong. I should have done a fancy meal, had a ring and got down on one knee, but Pip, I love you and as we walked across the street, your hand in mine, I knew that I didn't want to live another day—hell, not another minute—without you. I want it all. Marriage, a home, kids—"

My heart sank.

I hadn't told him about Amanda. And I'd never told him that in addition to never really loving Anthony the way I should, the idea of having children had been a problem.

When we were just neighbors, I hadn't owed him an explanation. Even when I realized we were good friends I didn't owe it to him. But now, I did. I'd owed him the explanation since Christmas and probably even before that. And I knew it.

Telling him had flitted around the edges of my mind, but I'd swatted the thought away each time it came within reach. Not that I thought he'd judge me.

I trusted Ned completely. I knew he'd support me and that decision I made so many years ago, but this wasn't a story to tell tonight.

He looked concerned and I realized that I'd hesitated too long.

"Pip, I thought you'd feel the same way," Ned said softly.

"I do," I assured him. "I may be a writer, but I don't have the words to tell you how much I love you. How much I love the life we're build-ing. And yes, we should move in together. As for the rest—"

"Marriage and kids?" he asked.

I nodded. "We need to talk about that. About . . ."

"About?" he pressed.

"Later? Could we talk about this later? It will be a longer conversa-tion than we can have right now."

He looked hurt.

Knowing that I'd been the one to put the pained look in his eyes hurt me as well. For the first time I'd hurt, or maybe disappointed, the man I loved. I kissed him, hoping to wipe away the feeling. "I love you, Ned. More than you can ever know. Can you wait until later for the rest?"

He sighed. "Pip, I'll wait as long as you need me to. I should never have brought this up tonight. So we'll table the discussion until later. Just know I love you. That will never change."

I did know that. And I realized just how amazing that was . . . to know that someone loved you so completely. Once upon a time, I'd worried about a spark, but what we had wasn't a spark, nor was it a blaze—something that would burn out as fast as it began. No, this was a well-tended fire that would burn steadily and warmly for the rest of my life.

My kids found us in our corner of the wing, and it was no longer quiet. Jo came up to me and squealed as she hugged me, and some of my excitement came roaring back.

Ned loved me and I loved him.

We'd work this out.

I was surrounded by the kids as the program started. The princi-pal of the school was first at the microphone and welcomed everyone to the event. He introduced my mom, in her capacity as superinten-dent. She walked onto the stage from the opposite backstage wing and smiled at me.

"Thank you, everyone, for coming out tonight. I'm here in two capacities. First, as superintendent it's my honor to be here and introduce the participants in this unique and wonderful project. But I'm also here as a mother. I'm so proud to introduce my daughter, Piper George, who not only spent months spearheading this project, but has also spent her entire adult life donating her time and talents in so many ways that benefit the community." Mom continued her short speech, talking about the project and the students who were involved. She finished by saying, ". . . So on behalf of the entire school district, I want to thank and congratulate Piper George. I'm going to turn the microphone over to her before I start blubbering up here and totally embarrass myself."

She waved to me and said, "Piper."

Ned squeezed my hand, then released it as I walked out onto the stage. I wiped at my eyes and kissed my mom as I reached her and the mic. She walked off the stage and I said, "Geesh, thanks, Mom, for worrying about blubbering and making a spectacle of yourself." I over-exaggerated as I wiped my eyes, trying to make the very necessary act funny.

"And I'm honored to be here speaking on behalf of everyone who was involved with *Raise Your Hands: Stories from Today's Classrooms*. But before I talk a bit about this very special project, I'd like to introduce the writers who were able to be with us tonight."

As I read their names, one by one the kids filed on to the stage and took one of the seats behind me. "And finally, the girl who inspired the project, Jo Larson. Jo's the only writer who's not currently a school district student. She's a freshman at Gannon University this year, but she took time away from her classes to not only write for the book, but also help with the project."

All the kids who'd written for the book stood as the audience applauded, and soon the entire auditorium was standing and applauding.

Jo's cheeks turned a brilliant red as she walked to the end of the seats. Soon the auditorium was quiet again and I turned back to the mic.

"I've been writing for years, and I can tell you that each current project is my favorite. If it's not, I'm doing something wrong. As I finish a book, I move on to the next one, which then becomes my new favorite.

"But *Raise Your Hands: Stories from Today's Classrooms* is a book that will forever have a firm place in my heart, not only because the stories are all amazing and give such a raw, honest look at today's classrooms, but because of the students had the opportunity to work. No, not students . . . writers. All of them opened themselves up and wrote from the heart. Their stories are ones that every educator should read. They're stories that every parent of a school-age student should read. Well, let's face it: I think everyone at every stage of his or her life should read this book."

That got a laugh.

"So please take a minute to talk to all our student writers tonight, and then go home and talk to the students in your life. Ask about their reality. It might be very different than you've imagined.

"I think that's it. I'm honored to have worked with these amazing kids, and I am anxious to see what the next chapter of their lives will look like. I'm sure it will be brilliant."

I started to walk off the stage, but Jo called my name and ran off the stage and came back wheeling a dolly with a huge potted bush on it. She stopped at the microphone and said, "We thought about buying Ms. Pip roses, but we all did some of our work in her garden and we decided we wanted to leave a mark on it. So we went to Johnston's nursery and they said you'd like this. Now, every time you look at it, you'll remember how much we appreciate everything you've done. Not just working with us on our book, but for all the books you've written. You write stories that don't talk down to kids . . . they tell the truth."

She hugged me and I finally did start crying.

Ned came out and wheeled my new bush off the stage because I could hardly see through my tears.

That night, after the book signing and party, I wrote in Amanda's journal.

Dear Amanda,

I've tucked a copy of every book I've ever written in that chest for you. Today, I added Raise Your Hands. It's special because I didn't write it. I edited it and maybe mentored it, but you're in it as much as you are in any of my other books. As I read all the kids' stories and worked with them, I thought of you. I wonder about your high school experience. As it comes to an end, are you sighing with relief, or are you sad to see this part of your life draw to a close?

I hope as you read this journal, whatever chapter of your life you're in is a good one.

Love,
Piper

Chapter Fourteen

Foreword from Raise Your Hands, by Piper George:

I started my career in pediatric nursing and fell into writing by accident. My first books were for younger readers, but the last few years I've started writing Young Adult fiction. When I meet readers and they tell me, "I thought you were my age," I'm so complimented.

I've spent most of my adult life trying to see the world from a child's, and then from a young adult's, perspective. More than see the world, I try to feel the world and be relevant as I write.

The student authors in this collection bring an authenticity that no matter how close I come I can never truly master. They bring a rawness, and in some cases a vulnerability, to their writing as they describe their school experiences. My hope is this book will help parents understand what it means to be a teen today, and that it will help student readers realize they're not alone. I hope it will make readers feel that some of their own experiences are captured in this story. Every child or young adult needs to feel that he or she has that connection and more importantly, that his or her voice is heard . . .

The next morning, I could not get going.

After the signing, a bunch of the students and their families had stopped by my house. At about eleven, Ned left for some stakeout. He was never very specific about his work projects, but he assured me he'd be safe.

Cooper stayed after everyone else had left. It was after one when I said good night to her.

Sundays are generally my lazy day, but sleeping in until eight o'clock in the morning went beyond lazy to crazy for me. I'm normally an early bird, but a late night and too much on my mind had made for a fitful night's sleep.

It wasn't helped by the fact that Ned had been gone all night. I kept waking up and reaching for him, only to find myself alone in my bed.

No, not *my* bed anymore. *Our* bed.

I took my coffee and paper out to the garden for the first time. The calendar said it was officially spring, and today, Mother Nature wasn't arguing.

I was wrapped in a quilt, because although the sun was out, there was still a nip in the air. This was Erie, Pennsylvania, after all.

I was studying the backyard, trying to decide where I could possible fit the new bush the kids had given me, when the gate opened.

For a moment, I thought it was Ned. I knew we needed to talk, but I'd been avoiding thinking about it. I wasn't sure how to start. *Hey, Ned, I haven't mentioned it before, but I have a kid . . . sort of.*

It wasn't Ned, but my mom who came into view. My always-dressed-to-the-nines mother was disheveled and it was obvious she'd been crying.

"Mom? What's wrong? Is it Dad?" I jumped up from the bench. "Did something happen to Dad?"

She shook her head and pulled me back onto the bench with her. "No. That's not it. Your father's still sleeping. I left to come over here before he woke up. I've been up all night. Your speech last night . . ."

She shook her head.

I opened up the quilt and wrapped her in it along with me.

We sat in silence, wrapped up together, while my mother collected herself.

"This book . . ."

"The book? I only wrote the foreword and afterword. It's the students' stories, not mine."

"Maybe not yours, but I know that as you worked on it, as you worked with those children, you saw Amanda. You saw her in every story, on every page, in every student. Piper, I read it in one sitting and when I finished, I started to cry. I haven't been able to stop."

"Mom?" I knew that some of the stories were tearjerkers, but I hadn't expected this reaction from anyone, much less my mother.

"I've always been behind you, always supported your philanthropic nature. But until last night, I don't think I ever realized that everything you've done, everything you do, has been for your daughter. For Amanda."

"It has," I admitted softly. "I may have given her up, but my life has been built around her. Someday, if or when she finds me, I want her to know that I never forgot her. Not for one minute of one day."

"That's what I realized last night. You're heartbroken and it's my fault," my mother—my strong, brash mother who'd always stood by my side and lent me her strength and support—whispered as she started to cry again.

Heartbroken?

I really thought hard before I answered. *Heartbroken?*

Giving up my child was the hardest thing I'd ever done. And I'd missed her every day since she left my arms and yes, I worried about her, in much the same way everyone who's ever had a child worries. Yes, I'd built a life around her. But my heart wasn't broken. Seventeen years later, I still believed I'd made the best decision for both of us. Surely I'd sent a piece of my heart with her when she left, but what was left was intact.

If it was broken, I couldn't have given it to Ned, and I was sure that I'd done that.

"Mom, that's not—" I started to protest.

She interrupted, "It is. I read the book. You might not have written every word in it, but your heart bled on the pages."

"Mom—"

She interrupted. "I am your mother." She wiped at her eyes. "My job is to save you from pain. And though you didn't talk about Amanda, I've always seen her clearly behind your stories. She was the little girl in the grocery store and the reason you started Amanda's Pantry. She's every child you've written for. She's Jo Larson and all the other students who worked on the book."

I didn't know what to say to all that, because it was true. "Where you see pain, I see—"

"I could have saved you all the pain if I hadn't been so selfish," she admitted. "I could have dropped out of my doctorate program. Juggling school and my teaching took so much time away from home— from you and your father. Even before the baby, I sensed how much strain it was putting on our relationship. You were at an age when you needed your mother present. If I had been around more, maybe you'd never have gotten pregnant. Maybe—"

"Mom, stop," I said in my firmest nurse's voice. I didn't need to use it often anymore, but I still had it. "I know you've always worried that I was somehow torturing myself, first by working on the ped's floor at the hospital, then with the books and Amanda's Pantry. And you've always been wrong. All the things I do give me such . . . satisfaction. Joy. No, glee."

My new character was a bubbly sort who used the word *glee* a lot. Sometimes I give characters attributes I want to develop, and sometimes I give them attributes I already have or believe in. I think most of my life is a quiet sort of happiness. Sitting here in my garden, reading a Sunday paper, or working on the front porch.

But those quiet, happy moments were punctuated by frequent moments of utter and absolute glee. Story times at the school when one of the kindergarteners hugs me. Saturdays at Amanda's Pantry. Letters from readers, or from people the pantry has helped. Other moments.

And Ned.

Always Ned.

It didn't matter if we were cooking dinner, or washing the dishes together. It didn't matter if we were walking the dogs, or weeding my backyard jungle.

Waking up next to him and watching him sleep.

Those were small moments that filled me with . . . definitely glee.

I realized my mother needed to hear that. So I repeated it and kept listing things. "Dinner with you and Dad. Seeing you win that award last year. Our vacation to the Outer Banks so many years ago. Do you remember the baby turtle?"

Her tears were slowing and she nodded. "You were so excited as we watched it crawl from the sand and into the water."

"*Glee*, Mom," I said, borrowing the word again. "My life is filled with the big moments and the smaller ones, but all of them make me happy. I need you to hear this and believe what I'm about to say this time. I have an utterly wonderful life."

"But—" she started.

I interrupted. "Mom, I would never have let you quit school to help me keep Amanda, because I'm sure in my heart of hearts, she's where she was supposed to be. She's with a couple who couldn't have biological children. She's loved and cherished. They were able to give her the childhood and life I wanted for her. Please hear me on this—I wouldn't have let you quit school to help with her because even if you could have been home more to be Amanda's grandmother, *I* wasn't equipped to be her mother. Not the kind of mother I dreamed of for her. No matter what, I'd have still given her up for adoption. It was the right thing for her. For me. And for you." I wrapped my arm around her. "Honestly, Mom, it was the right thing."

She fell silent. I knew her well enough to simply sit quietly next to her and allow her a moment to digest what I'd said.

After a few minutes, I quietly added, "You were the best mother ever. I was too young to live up to that, and that was what I wanted for Amanda. I truly believe that's what I gave her. And I'm at peace with the decision. I always have been. I won't say I never worry about her. I think we worry about people we love, which is why you're here this morning, worrying about me."

"Still, what if I—"

"Ned has pointed out that I use *what if* every day when I work, but you have to be fair. What if you had quit and I tried to raise her? Could I still have made it through college? Would I still have been a nurse? And if I weren't, would I have become a writer? Or would I have started Amanda's Pantry? If I hadn't started Amanda's Pantry, what would happen to all the kids and families we serve? Mom, maybe I'm the selfish one, but like I said, I love my life. All the work I do is filled with meaning, and I'm surrounded by people I love."

"Ned," she said.

This time I didn't answer but only nodded.

"Have you told him about Amanda then?"

"No. I really don't know why. I know he'll accept that part of me, just like he's accepted every other part of me. It's just . . ."

"Just?" Mom prompted.

"What if he sees me differently?" There. I'd given my hesitancy a name.

I think I'd known all along this was a big part of why I hadn't told him. "I mean, if I can't convince you that I'm at peace with my past, and that I love my life as it stands, how can I convince him? What if he sees me as a tragic figure and pities me?"

Mom sat straighter and all traces of her tears disappeared in an instant. "You're right. I've done you a disservice seeing you as someone who's heartbroken. Giving away a piece of your heart doesn't break it. A heart never runs out of room. A heart can always expand. You gave a part to Amanda, and you've given pieces to every child you've worked with at the hospital, the pantry, and at the school. You put a piece of your heart in every book you write . . . that's what your readers respond to. Your stories are genuine because you put yourself into them."

"I try to," I admitted.

"You've given away all those pieces of your heart, but instead of having less left, your heart's only gotten bigger because of it. You need to tell Ned, and he'll see that."

I'd meant what I'd said; I wasn't afraid of him not accepting me after learning what happened all those years ago, but I was afraid that somehow he'd see me differently.

Still, I had to tell him. We couldn't go any further until I did.

Dear Amanda,

When I picked up this soft leather notebook the first time, it was a book of blank pages. I thought I would fill those pages with a part of your story you never knew. A part you could never know unless I told it to you in this journal, and the chest full of letters, pictures, and even a few receipts that I've kept from Amanda's Pantry.

For almost four years, I've worked on your story. Only, I've come to realize that part of your story is my story. This journal, or letter, is autobiographical in nature. Your autobiography and mine. As if that symbiotic union we shared for nine months wasn't severed at your birth, or even when your parents took you from my arms and walked out of my life with you.

Now, as most of the pages of the journal are filled, I've realized it's even more than just our story—it's the story of all the people whose lives we've touched. It's their stories, too. At least a chapter or a few pages of their stories.

For instance, though I only ever caught a glimpse of your parents, it's their story in a way.

I've rarely mentioned your biological father, but yes, it's his as well. He was a boy, as much as I was a girl, when you were conceived. He walked away from the news, still very much a boy, while I was forced to grow up in that instant I realized you existed. I was forced to make decisions for you that would affect your entire life.

I don't resent your father's ability to stay Peter Pan. Maybe he grew up a few years later, or maybe he grew up yesterday.

Or maybe he's never grown up.

I don't begrudge him the time he remained a child.

Nor would I change my instant move from childhood to adulthood, because my transformation sent you into your parents' arms and into what I pray was a happy life.

Today, I realized how very much our story is my mother's story, too.

My mother thought my heart was broken because I'd given you to your parents.

It wasn't.

It isn't.

And I think she finally understood. My mother was almost poetic as she realized that hearts are unique. You can give away piece after piece, but there's always more. I sent a piece of my heart away with you. I've given other pieces to the kids I've worked with over the years. And yet, rather than getting smaller, my heart continues to expand and grow. I've given a huge part of it to Ned now, and yet there's still more.

And that, Amanda, is why this journal isn't just for me or you. It's about and for all the people we've both touched.

In the trunk you'll find a letter from your grandmother.

I meant what I said to her. Even if she'd offered to quit school, I'd have still given you up for adoption because I truly believed it was what was best for you. And maybe that's the sign of a good parent, doing what's best for your child no matter how it hurts.

Maybe that's part of what I've done since you left . . . tried to grow up to be the parent I wanted to be then, the parent you deserved, so that if you ever find me, you'll find a woman you can be proud of.

And I hope that if you find me you realize that I loved you enough to let you go.

As I finish this entry, I realize that this story is Ned's story, too, though he doesn't know it yet. It's his because . . . I love him. And we're connected. So he's part of my story, and thus part of your story.

Tomorrow, I'm going to tell him about you.

I've told him so many things—shared so much of myself with him. Why haven't I told him about you? Why don't I tell the world about you, about how much I love you?

I don't tell the world because that's not my right. I gave that right away when I handed you over to your real parents.

Part of the reason I haven't told Ned is that I don't want him to see me differently or feel sorry for me.

I know that you used to stand alone at the core of my heart, and so many others orbited around you. But you're no longer alone there . . . Ned's there, too. And I trust him enough to share you with him.

Love,
Piper

As I wrote those words, I realized that right there at the center of my being with Amanda was Ned.

He was at the center of my heart, standing next to Amanda, and everyone and everything else I loved circled them—orbited around them.

Maybe it's all about perspective. For the longest time he was simply Ned.

My neighbor.

My dog co-parent.

My sci-fi buddy.

My friend.

Finally, part of my family.

And now?

I felt as if I'd climbed on a *Dead Poets Society* desk and was looking at Ned from a new perspective and there was only one conclusion I could reach.

I loved him and had loved him for a very long time.

I'd said the words for months, but as I weighed and measured what he was to me, the word *love* carried more weight.

I let it play on my lips—love—discovering the taste and texture of it. I told him at Christmas that I loved him and I meant it, but I realized how much deeper my feelings had grown.

Ned was integral to my life . . . to my happiness.

He was as much a part of me as breathing or eating.

He hadn't been back to his house to spend a night since Christmas. I loved going to bed with him at my side. I loved waking up next to him.

I loved making coffee for us in the morning, then sharing it with him.

I loved walking the dogs with him at night.

He was a part of me in a way that no one other than Amanda had ever been.

I've loved many things with varying degree of feeling.

For instance, I love ice cream, but it is a very different feeling than my love for say, Bruce and Princess. Or the love I feel for my work. The love for the kids I work with. My love for my parents.

My love for Amanda.

Amanda had lived in the center of my heart for seventeen years. Now, Ned was there, too.

Chapter Fifteen

Ned finally came home. His exhaustion was evident in the way he placed his feet with care, as if he might fall over if he didn't.

He smiled when he saw me and said, "Hey, you."

In a fluid motion he took off his coat, hung it on a hook, then pulled me into his arms and kissed me good morning, which was not really good morning, but by now was good afternoon.

He didn't release, but held me close. I rested my head on his chest and asked, "Did you find your guy?"

He nodded. "Finally."

Now that I'd made up my mind to tell Ned, I wanted to simply do it. But he was exhausted—too tired for me to spring this on him.

But Ned, being Ned, sensed my need. "What?" he asked.

"I have something to tell you, but it can wait until after you've slept." I'd waited well past the time I should have told him, and a few more hours wouldn't make any difference.

He stared at me a minute, as if I were an open book and he was reading every line. "No, I don't think it can."

He took my hand and led me to the couch.

As we sat down, I remembered that first day. Couch Couch was a perceptive man. He smiled, encouraging me to share whatever I needed to share with him.

"Ned, I . . ."

How to tell him? I'd had plenty of time to think about the best way, but I hadn't.

I could ease into it. I could fill in the backstory first. There were so many ways of getting to the truth of it, but I didn't take any of those longer routes. Instead, I jumped right into it. "I have a daughter."

I watched as that smile melted into something else. It was an expression I couldn't quite define. Curiosity? Shock? Concern?

He didn't say anything for a time as he digested my statement. I waited, giving him a moment to adjust his reality to include the fact that I had a daughter.

"Amanda?" he half stated and half asked.

I nodded.

"She lives with her father?" he asked slowly.

I twisted the string of my sweatshirt around my finger and I shook my head. "With her *mother* and father. At least, I hope with her mother and father."

He didn't say anything for a minute. I apologized. "I'm making a mess of this," I said.

Ned shook his head and looked confused. "I still don't understand."

"I know. Let me start at the beginning. I was fifteen when I got pregnant and barely sixteen when I had Amanda. I couldn't be the mother she deserved so I gave her up for adoption." I offered him a small smile.

"Do you know her?"

I shook my head. "No. It wasn't an open adoption."

"But you know her name?" he pressed.

"No, not the name her parents gave her, but to me, she's always been Amanda. It really does mean 'worthy of love.' I looked it up in a baby book while I was pregnant. And she's that." I thought of the baby I'd cradled in my arms for that one short hour. She'd been all peach fuzz and sweetness, and oh so worthy of being loved. "Of all the things I've hoped for her, that's the biggest one. That she found a loving home."

"And her father?" He paused and corrected himself. "Amanda's father?"

For one passing moment, I hoped that Mick had indeed grown up into a better person than he'd seemed to be when I'd told him. "He denied that the baby could be his, even though we both knew it couldn't be anyone else's." I sighed. "He was only a kid. I'd like to think he'd handle things differently now."

"*You* were only a kid." Ned willingly left the subject of Amanda's father behind and said, "I asked you about your dedications, and you brushed off my question. Did you think it would change how I felt about you? Even before we were a couple and were just friends? Did you think I'd judge you? All these years, you've never said anything."

"Ned, I need you to understand, I've known that when I told you—and honestly, it seems like I've always known I would tell you—that you'd accept her. That you'd accept me. That you'd support me." I took a deep breath and admitted what I'd only just come to realize myself. "I didn't want you to pity me. Or see me as broken or haunted by Amanda's loss. My mother always has and I hated it. I didn't want you to see me differently."

"Pip, I will always see you as simply you. Unique and wonderful," he said and opened his arms. For a long while he held me . . . simply held me.

"Only my parents and my Aunt Bonnie ever knew about her. No one else. Not Coop, not my editor, not anyone who's ever asked who the Amanda from the pantry or from my books was."

"Never any of the other men you've dated?" he asked.

I knew he was asking about Anthony. "There haven't been many men, but no, not even Anthony. If I'd loved him, I'd have told him."

That was a truth I'd come to accept. "I never did love him, so no matter what, things would still have ended with us."

"But you knew you'd tell me?" Ned asked carefully.

"Because I love you. Ned, I think I've always loved you. I'm not sure how I thought what I felt was less than it is. I know, that doesn't make sense. But here's the thing, Amanda's always been at the center of my heart and I realize she's not there alone. She hasn't been for a long time. I love you."

He held me for the longest time. I didn't cry, though I might have. There was no passionate kiss, just Ned holding me and saying with that contact that he accepted what I'd given him. He'd accepted my trust along with my heart.

"You have a daughter," he murmured quite a while later.

As he said the words, I realized they weren't true. "I know that's what I said, but truly I'm just the woman who gave birth to her."

"And you are the woman who loves her, if your dedications in all those books are accurate."

"They are, and I do love her, sight unseen. Well, not exactly unseen. I insisted that I get one hour with her after I gave birth. They cleaned her up and handed her to me. She was swaddled, but I unwrapped her. She had ten perfect toes on two very long and skinny feet. I'm afraid I gave her my feet, which was not the best gift I could have given her."

"What's wrong with your feet?" Ned asked. He sounded as if he was insulted on my feet's behalf.

I held them up for him. "They're big. When I was young, having big feet was the bane of my existence."

"*The Hunt for Bigfoot and Other Wonders of the Eighth Grade?*" he asked, naming the slightly autobiographical book.

"Yes. I based it on me. Well, at least I based her feet on my feet." His question had given me a moment to pull myself together.

I went back to those precious sixty minutes. "I counted Amanda's fingers. I looked at her umbilical cord, which was clamped. It was impossible to tell if it was going to be an innie or an outie. I was hoping for an innie for her.

"I studied her hair. It was very fine and there was a reddish hue to it." I fingered a strand of my own hair. "I hope that the color settled in more of a brown or blond zone and her hair is tamer than mine."

He picked up a strand of my crazy hair and said, "I like your hair."

"You like me, so you're biased." I kissed his cheek and then continued, "I tried to memorize her. When I was done, I rewrapped her, and then I sang her every lullaby I knew. '*Rock-a-bye Baby*,' only I changed up the line about the cradle falling and the baby coming down to *and Mama will catch you, cradle and all*. And then I cried with the realization that I wouldn't be the mother catching her. Some other woman would. But as I cried, I continued singing. '*Close Your Eyes.*' '*Sweet Baby James.*' And as the minutes ticked by, and there were only a few more spins around the dial left, I told her how much I loved her. I told her that no matter where she went or what she did, my love was a constant. My love. I'd written her a letter for when she was older. I didn't seal it. I wanted her parents to be able to read it. I'm sure they'd want to check it and me out. But I tucked my great-grandmother's locket into it. My great-grandmother Rose was so strong, and I wanted Amanda to know she came from a family of very strong women."

"You gave her a piece of her history."

I nodded. "There, in the locket, was a picture of Rose and her husband. The photos were small, but I always thought you could see the love between them. I wanted to give her a slice of her family history and let her see that when we love, we love completely. That's how I loved her—completely. And I wrote a note to her parents, asking them to give her the letter when they thought she was old enough."

"And that was it?" he asked.

I nodded. "When the hour was up, I kissed her one last time. The nurse carried her away. The door was still open and as I saw the nurse put Amanda in the other woman's arms, I called, *Good-bye, Amanda.*"

"You loved her and you *named* her."

"I knew that no one but me would ever use that name, but I had to be able to call her something when I thought about her. And I knew I would think about her. I believed that the raging ache would eventually subside."

"Did it?" he asked.

"Yes. The ache subsided. I still miss her, which sounds odd." I paused and added, "My mother was here earlier today. She'd read the new book in one sitting and was blaming herself. She thought she should have quit her doctorate program and helped me so I could have kept Amanda. I tried to make her see that I showed my daughter how much I loved her by giving her the best chance at the type of childhood I'd had. The kind of parents I'd had. I wasn't ready to be the kind of parent mine were. I tried to make Mom understand, and I want you to understand that I miss Amanda, but I'm at peace with the decision. Sometimes, I worry about her. But that's what people do—they worry about the people they love."

Ned nodded as if he truly understood. And I didn't doubt that he did.

"When you said you wanted to sell your house and move in, I was thrilled. Then you started to talk about marriage and kids." I shook my head. "I was going to tell you about Amanda no matter what, but you need to know now why I can say, *yes, move in with me.* I can even say, *yes, I'll marry you.* But Ned, I can't have other children. While I'm at peace with that decision I made so many years ago, I hope with all my heart that someday Amanda comes to find me. And when she does, I won't have her wondering why I had and kept other children, but not her. I can't have her think that somehow I loved them more."

I'd set Amanda's journal out on the table earlier. I picked it up and handed it to him.

"Your bear trap," he said as he took it.

I nodded. "I wrote it for her. I've never shown it to anyone else, but I'd like you to read it. I've filled almost all the pages. The timing seems apt. She'll be graduating soon. So, I'll finish the book and tuck it away with everything else I have for her, and I'll wait. I'd like to have you waiting with me."

Ned sat up, putting a bit of distance between us. Seconds passed. He held the journal and simply looked at me. It felt as if I was an open book and he could peruse me at will.

Finally he gave a slight nod, as if he had found whatever he'd been looking for.

"Pip, I've always known you were strong and that you had the biggest heart of anyone I'd ever met, but I didn't imagine the depths of that strength or the size of your heart."

"I don't think I'm strong, but I guess I was strong enough," I said. Yes. I'd been strong enough to do what was right.

"At sixteen you had the strength to do what was right for Amanda, not for yourself. It's another reason why I love you. As for marriage—"

"I want to marry you," I told him again. I did. More than anything I'd ever wanted. "But I have to be clear on the issue of children. I need you to understand that I won't have any more."

"Given the circumstances, I think Amanda would realize that you gave her to parents who could raise her because you loved her."

"But what if she doesn't? What if she comes to find me and finds I have a houseful of children to love? What if I can't make her understand? I can't take that chance."

"Pip—" he said.

Just my name. I could hear the pain in his voice and knew that the idea of not having children hurt him. He'd be a great father. He'd be the kind of dad who'd be there for his kids. He'd go to their school activities, read them bedtime stories. He'd make them a priority.

He deserved to have a big family.

A family I couldn't—maybe wouldn't—give him. "Ned, I—"

He held the journal in his hand.

"I'll understand if you want to back out," I said. "You want kids and I see—"

He snorted and shook his head. "No, you don't see anything if you can't see that I'd rather have you than any yet-to-be-conceived children." He leaned down and kissed me. "I love you, Pip. And you love me. I know that. And I know you in a way most men will never know the women they love."

I shook my head.

"I have read every book you've ever written. I'll read Amanda's journal. But now that I know about her, I realize every book you've written has been for her. I can see her—and I can see your love for her—in every page. I know you, Pip. And I love you enough to wait for you to figure things out."

"Don't go into this thinking I'll change my mind on the having children issue," I warned him. "I'm being honest when I say I won't. I live in hope that someday Amanda will come find me. I've put my name on the adoption registries, so it shouldn't be too hard for her to find me. I need to know I made the right decision. That she was happy. And I need her to understand why I made that decision. I won't have her hurt by because I've had other children and kept them."

"I can't imagine that's how she'd feel," he said.

"I make my living imagining. And I've played that scene over and over again in my mind. Maybe you're right and she would be thrilled to have siblings. I know that's a possibility."

"But maybe I'm wrong?" he asked gently.

I nodded. "I can't take that chance. I want to say yes to your proposal, but I need to be sure that you understand."

"Like I said, I understand you better than you understand yourself. I get it. Right now, though, I need some sleep."

"I knew this should have waited until after—"

"No, you're wrong. It shouldn't have waited another minute. Is it okay if I crash here, or would you rather I go home so you don't have to tiptoe around the house?"

"It's up to you," I said. What I wanted to say was, *Stay. Don't ever leave.*

"I'll be back over after I get some sleep." He kissed me and then left. Just walked out of my door with Amanda's journal in his hand.

For the last four years, I'd written to Amanda after so many big and small moments.

I knew the pages were almost filled, and I'd told myself that when it was full, I'd be done.

But right now, I wanted to write to her. I'd tried to explain things to her in the journal before, but I wanted to try again. Maybe try to explain myself better to her than I'd explained myself to Ned.

I loved him.

And I wasn't sure that was going to be enough.

Chapter Sixteen

The next few weeks were awkward.

Ned didn't mention marriage or families . . . or Amanda. He also didn't mention having read the journal, but one day after he left for another outing, I found it in the center of the bed.

I picked it up and sat cross-legged in front of the faded blue trunk. I traced the *T. P. E. 1837*.

Talia Piper Eliason. I wondered what this woman I'd been named after was like. And then I thought about Rose. Rose who'd sent her son away to a better life.

What would her son have said if he'd met her again? Would he have thanked her for her sacrifices? Would he have blamed her because he'd grown up feeling the lack of a mother in his life?

I thought about writing in the journal, but for the first time in four years, I didn't know what to say to Amanda. I gently placed it in the trunk, along with all the books and letters—all the pieces of Amanda's story—and I shut the lid.

I stood and looked out the window at my garden. Everything was blooming. It was that fresh, spring green that would deepen over the summer, until turning into a tired green by fall. I thought about going out back, but even that didn't appeal. Nothing felt right.

I needed to fix things with Ned, but I didn't know how. He was out of town somewhere again, so I wouldn't be fixing anything today.

I knew that although he still said he loved me, our relationship had shifted when I told him about Amanda. I just wasn't sure what it was shifting to.

He felt distant. But maybe it was me. Maybe I was pulling back in order to protect myself.

Ned claimed he knew me, but if he did, he'd know how much this awkwardness between us was hurting me.

To really stir my jumbled emotional pot, it was Mother's Day.

Despite having had a daughter, I knew that I wasn't a mother. That knowledge had always made Mother's Day one of the hardest days of the year for me.

As I had so many other years, I decided to concentrate on my mom. I took my parents down to Smuggler's Wharf, a lovely little restaurant that sat on the bay.

Dad talked about his classes and his book. I listened and nodded at the proper places.

I realized my mother sensed my mood when she reached across the table and took my hand. "Piper . . ." That's all she said, my name, but I knew she was telling me she was sorry and that she understood. I'm pretty sure that for the first time she understood that it wasn't regret that made the day hard, it was simply missing Amanda.

How could I miss someone I'd only held for an hour? I wasn't sure, but I did.

I gave Mom's hand a squeeze and wondered about the woman Amanda called mom.

I looked at my mother and hoped that Amanda's was like her. Strict, but reasonable. Loving. Always so loving. And understanding.

After lunch, we drove from the bay to the peninsula and took a long walk. My mother always swore she was a simple soul. A day when she didn't have to cook and got a trip to Presque Isle was enough to celebrate any holiday in her mind.

We stayed for the sunset. As it lowered in the sky, I felt the pulse of missing Amanda with each breath I took. Maybe it was amplified because I missed Ned, too. Not just because he'd been traveling so much, but because I felt as if the distance between us grew wider every day.

Ned and Amanda.

Amanda and Ned.

"Piper," my mother said again.

She wrapped her arm around me as we stood, watching the sun sink into Lake Erie.

My father seemed oblivious to my turmoil, which was fine with me. I thought maybe I'd go write in the journal, but my parents had barely pulled out of my driveway when Ned came in the door.

"Happy Mother's Day, Pip," he said as he handed me the flowers. He had a bouquet of flowers in his hand. Forget-me-nots and white roses—my favorites.

And out of nowhere I felt a burst of anger flare in my chest. "I am not a mother. I gave up that name years ago when I gave up my daughter."

Even as I said the words, I realized that calling Amanda my daughter when I'd always denied being a mother—being *her* mother—didn't make sense.

Ned didn't call me out on the contradiction. He simply pulled me into his arms and said, "You are most definitely a mother."

"I gave Amanda away and gave that name to another woman."

"Pip, you know that I think your mother's great. She reminds me of my mom in so many ways. And do you know what quality shines through in both of them? The thing that makes them such outstanding mothers?"

When I didn't respond, he said, "A good mother—like both of our mothers—is someone who puts her own wants and needs aside in the interest of her child."

I still didn't say anything. He didn't need me to agree to something we both knew to be true.

"If that's the definition of a mother, then you have been a mother since before Amanda was even born. You gave her up—gave up that piece of your heart—so that she could have a better life. You've missed her ever since."

He held my hand and allowed me to simply mull over his words.

After a long time, my hand still in his, he said, "You are a mother. You've always been one, Pip." He let go of my hand, leaned down, and picked up the slightly banged-up flowers. "And every Mother's Day from now on, I will bring you flowers on Amanda's behalf. If she knew what you'd done for her, she'd bring them herself."

He was quiet again, giving me time to compose myself and more than that, time to let what he said really sink in.

"I am Amanda's mother." I'd never said those words before. In my heart, she'd always been my daughter, but I'd never allowed myself to think of myself as her mother. I'd always forced myself to think of her other mother as her mother. I was simply the woman who'd given birth to her and then given her away.

She'd been my daughter, but I'd never been her mother.

Until now.

Until Ned.

That was a greater gift than any flowers.

It was the best Mother's Day present I'd ever received.

"Thank you," I whispered. And this time, I didn't wait for him to pull me into his arms. I walked into them willingly. I stepped into his embrace and knew that he'd open his arms to me.

And he did.

I wasn't sure we'd settled anything, but I knew he loved me. I knew I loved him.

And for now, that would be enough.

Dear Amanda,

Sharing biographical stats with someone is easy. Your name, the city you were born in, what high school you went to, jobs . . . all those things I can share with ease. I share them with readers and friends alike.

But getting to your truths . . . those pieces of yourself that you keep hidden from sight because they're so fragile that an unkind word or scathing look could damage them—damage you—is so much harder.

Amanda, that's why I started this journal. I hope and dream that someday we'll meet. I can tell you my blood type, my family's medical history. I can even give you some cursory information along those lines about your father. And maybe that's all you'll want from me. But I hope you want more. You've been part of my daily life since the moment I learned I was pregnant. We might not be together, but your existence has shaped and formed me. It has sent me in directions I might never have gone.

If all you want is those statistics, I will happily share them. But I will give you this journal and the chest of letters from people you helped. And maybe through them, you'll know more about me . . . about the things I hold closest and dearest to me. And you should know, of all those things, you are at the center.

There are only a couple of pages left in the journal.

But once, before I tuck this journal away in the chest, I want to sign an entry the way I feel. Not to take anything away from your mom, but to express what Ned finally drove home for me.

Love,
Your Other Mother

Chapter Seventeen

Ned and I settled into a new normal after Mother's Day. And though we didn't talk about it anymore, we lived together.

He put his house on the market, but we still we didn't talk about engagements or marriage or future children.

We fell back into our routine. I should have been happy. It seemed I had what I wanted—Ned with no strings or expectations.

And yet, I wasn't happy at all. I felt like we'd lost something. Maybe the sense of possibility. I'd cut off an entire potential future for us.

Ned was still gone more than he'd ever been. Not just local stake-outs, but gone out of town. He called every night while he was away, but I missed him so much I ached with it. My writing had suffered this spring. For the first time in my writing career, I'd had to ask my editor for an extension on this contract. I tried to force the words, but they wouldn't come.

I didn't sit on the porch in the mornings because if I did, I simply stared at my laptop screen. I felt like a fraud.

I'd helped out at the clinic a few days, read at the school and gone through the motions at the pantry, but for the first time, I felt disconnected from everything I did that gave my life meaning.

I felt lost.

On Monday afternoon, I heard someone at the screen door and knew Ned was home.

As I had the thought, he walked in.

I drank in the sight of him. "You're home. I've missed you . . ." Words came tumbling out of my mouth, one after another. None of them what I really wanted to say. *I love you. Ask me again to marry you, please.*

Ned hugged me, but I could tell that things had shifted again and I wasn't sure why or how now. I let my arms drop to my sides and stepped back. "Is something wrong?"

"No, not wrong," he said. "I did something, and I hope when you find out you'll understand why and forgive me for going behind your back."

"What did you do?" I asked.

Rather than answer, he said, "I have something for you," and thrust a DVD jewel case toward me.

I had no clue what he could possibly need me to see. I stood there, frozen, a DVD in my hand, and the man I loved was standing so close that I could smell his cologne. It smelled woodsy. Ourdoorsy. It smelled just the way Couch Couch might have smelled.

I must have stood there too long because Ned shook me from my musings by asking, "Can we watch it now, Pip?"

I smiled, though I wanted nothing more than to go back into his arms. Maybe, if he held me long enough, I could say all the things I needed to say. "It's your show."

"No, it's yours," was his cryptic response.

I put the DVD in and he sat on the couch next to me as I turned on the television, then hit play on the remote.

It was a graduation. I paused and looked at him. "I don't understand."

"Watch."

The camera panned to the aisle and students, wearing their blue-and-white caps and gowns, strolled into view. Only a couple kids walked by before I saw her.

I hit pause. There she was, frozen on my screen. I knew it was her in the same way my heart knew it was Ned on the other side of the door. Amanda.

Her hair had never faded to a browner shade. It was red, but not as crazy red as mine. I'd call it more strawberry blond. But red. She smiled in that frame I'd frozen on the screen.

Oh, she smiled so hard it looked as if her face might break from all the happiness that was trying to spill out.

She had different colored cords draped over her gown.

"You found her?" I didn't know how to feel. Thrilled to see her. Angry that Ned had gone looking for her.

"I didn't say anything to her or her parents," Ned said quickly. "I know I overstepped, but you needed to know. I've watched you write in that journal since I met you. And now I've read it. You needed not just to hope she was all right, but to see it. To be able to feel it in the depths of your bones."

I didn't know what to say to that.

"I found her a couple weeks ago. I was just going to give you a report, and a few pictures. But when I realized I could go to her graduation and film her and no one would be the wiser, I knew I had to. No one would know. I'd be just one more family member with a camera in his hand. I didn't know when I went just how much the camera would capture."

"What do you mean?" I asked.

"You'll have to watch. I couldn't do it justice if I tried to tell you," he said.

"I was willing to wait and hope . . ." I was crying so hard I couldn't say anything else. I stared at the screen again. There. Amanda.

She looked so utterly happy. And beautiful. And the cords meant she'd done well in high school.

Tears were streaming down my face. I didn't attempt to stop them or even brush them aside.

Ned said, "I know you were waiting for her. You would have waited forever. And I believed you when you said you did what was best for her, but you still worried. We've talked about you making your living from your imagination. That *what-if* is a tool of your trade. Every book you write is a *what-if* scenario for Amanda. What if she's bullied in school? What if her feet are big and she feels ugly? What if she's hurt, or scared, or unhappy? What if she was hungry or lost? I wanted to give you peace of mind while you wait for her."

"So you found her and went to her graduation." It was more a statement than a question.

"I found her so you would know she was okay. And if she wasn't—" Ned paused. "We'd have crossed that bridge together."

"Why?" I asked.

"Do you have to ask?"

I didn't have to ask. I saw his answer in his eyes. More than that, I felt it. It was such a deep, intimate part of me. It had always been there. Even this last month or so when things had felt off-kilter, it had been there. He loved me and I loved him.

I hit play on the remote again.

"You can fast-forward through the speeches," Ned said.

I shook my head no. I wanted to see this—to see every moment. I watched with more intensity than I'd ever watched anything.

The class slowly walked down the aisle and took their seats. A few didn't sit in the auditorium seats, but instead walked onto the stage and joined the teachers on the folding chairs up there.

Amanda was one of those.

The principal talked, but I heard none of the words. I lived for the moments the camera panned toward the chairs and I caught sight of her. As he filmed the scene, Ned must have known that's how I'd feel, because the camera didn't stray from her for long.

The first speaker talked, but to my ears it was *blah, blah, blah*. Amanda stood.

"What did they say?" I asked.

"She's valedictorian," Ned said quietly.

I hit rewind and went back and listened closely as they announced the valedictorian . . . Amanda. Only that wasn't her name. I'd always known that wasn't her name, but it was the name I'd carried with me through all those years of not knowing, of hoping, of praying for her.

Siobhan Ahearn.

She looked as Irish as her name sounded. It fit her.

I thought I saw my father in her. Ned had zoomed the camera in on her and yes, her eyes were my father's eyes. Eyes that I'd always thought looked like the picture of my great-grandmother Rose.

Amanda didn't look nervous as she stood at the podium in front of a microphone. I had never given a speech without practically quaking in my shoes, but I saw no evidence of that in her. I was impressed by her bravery.

But Amanda—Siobhan—looked as if she was as comfortable at the microphone as she was on her living room couch.

"Congratulations to all of us," she said and the room erupted in thunderous applause.

"We did it. We're graduating. I know that the last thing you all want to do is sit through a long speech. You've all gone to school with me for years . . . you've heard just about everything I have to say. I know, I've always had a lot to say." There was a pregnant pause, and as if on cue, the crowd laughed. She went on, "So I'll make this brief."

Someone in the audience shouted, "No, you won't."

The audience laughed again and Amanda-Siobhan laughed along with them.

But the noise died down and she grew more serious as she went back to her speech.

"Today we've reached a milestone and a crossroad. We are no longer children. We are adults and we all have decisions to make . . . important decisions that will affect the rest of our lives. Some of those decisions we already made or are in the process of making. Should we go to *X* school or *Y* school? Should we go to a trade school? Should we . . . ?"

She paused, then repeated, "Should we . . . ?" She left the sentence hanging there and toyed with her necklace.

I paused the DVD and tried to catch my breath.

"What?"

I'd been crying as I watched, but this was too much. I cried so hard I could hardly breathe past the tears.

"Pip?" Ned said, and I could hear that I was causing him pain, and that was enough to help me get myself back under control.

"The locket she's wearing. It's from me. The one I put in with the letter I wrote her and enclosed with a letter I wrote to her parents."

"What did the letter say?" Ned asked.

I'd kept copies of both letters for myself. I had read them both over the years, just to be sure that I'd said everything right. They almost felt like a story I told myself. I could quote them verbatim to Ned.

"I told her parents, 'Thank you. Thank you for taking my daughter into your home and into your heart. When, and if, you think she's ready, I've sent a letter to her along with a locket that was my grandmother's. I've left it unsealed so you can read it. If you choose not to give it to her, I understand. And even then, I thank you.'"

"You were a writer even then," Ned said. "And the letter to her?"

"It said, 'Please don't ever feel I gave you to your parents because I didn't love you or want you. I am too young, and you deserve so much more than I could give you. I would give you the sun and the moon; I would give you the world if I could, and still it wouldn't be enough. I love you so much, I wonder that my heart can hold so much feeling and still beat.

"I wanted to give you something tangible. This locket was my great-grandmother's. Two greats for you. Rose was an amazing lady. Her family was poor. She did what was expected. She married. Two months after she had her son, she lost her husband. Rather than raise her son, my grandfather, in poverty, she did the unexpected. She moved them to Dublin, where she worked as a maid in a hotel. But when he was five, she realized that wasn't enough. So again, she did something unexpected.

"She put his needs first. She packed his bag, gave him this locket with her picture and his father's, and sent him with an older sister to America. My grandfather never saw his mother again. But she worked and sent money for his upkeep and his education.

"His mother died when he was seventeen. He went on and became a teacher. When I was little, Grandpa used to tell me stories of his mom. He'd tell me about her strength. And I must have inherited enough of that strength to let you go. To give you a better life than I could give you. So if you wear the locket, remember, you come from a long line of people who are strong and who love deeply. Remember you have always been loved."

Ned was crying now, but managed to whisper, "God, Pip."

"I wanted her to know that sometimes love means letting go. I needed her to know that I loved her. I called on the strength of my Great-Grandmother Rose when I signed those adoption papers and gave my daughter to someone else to raise."

There on the screen was my daughter, holding on to Rose's locket.

"She knows," Ned said. "She knows."

I hoped so.

I hit play and Siobhan dropped the locket and said, "There are so many choices. And each one we make will have a lifelong impact. I know about that kind of life-changing decision. You see, today I need to thank both of my mothers for the choices they made. I thank the mother who raised me. She opened her heart and her home to a child she didn't give birth to. That decision—made before I was born—set my life on a path. Never has any child been so loved.

"But I also need to thank the mother who gave birth to me. Most of you don't know I'm adopted. Why would you? But before I was my parents' daughter, there was another woman who carried me for nine months."

She paused and I could see tears in her eyes even as I felt my own tears still streaming down my face. "She reached a crossroad in her life and made a decision that affected us both. She gave me my parents and because she did, she gave me a very happy life."

I paused the tape again. It was too much to take in all at once. I looked at Ned and hiccupped through my tears as I asked, "She was happy?"

Having only seen the few moments of her on my television, I thought she was, but I needed to hear him say it. I needed to know that she was.

Ned nodded. "From everything I found, she has been very happy. Her parents love her and she loves them. She's an only child who was doted on, but not spoiled. You gave her that, Pip. She had the life you dreamed of."

I brushed at my eyes, needing a clear view as I hit play. There she was, on the screen in front of me. "I hope that mother who gave birth to me and had the strength to give me to another couple to raise had an equally happy life.

"I've always known I was adopted, and I've wondered about my birth parents. For my graduation, Mom and Dad gave me a letter this other mother wrote for me. It had this locket in it." She touched the locket again. "And she told a beautiful story. I had my answer. Love. That other mother gave me away out of love. Someday, when I'm older, I will find her, if she wants to be found. And when I do, I'll say, *Thank you for your decision. That decision you made before I was born gave me a wonderful life.*"

Again, I hit pause because the tears were blinding me. I was crying too hard to watch anything more.

I cried for the great-grandmother who'd made an equally hard decision so many years ago.

I cried for the girl I was. A scared, heartbroken girl who spent one single hour with her daughter, then lived the next eighteen years building a life around the child she gave away.

I cried and Ned held me. He didn't say anything. He simply wrapped me in his arms and let me cry.

Finally, I pulled back, leaving Ned's shoulder soaked in my tears. He took the remote control, looked at me, and when I nodded, he hit play.

Siobhan said, "When I find that mother who gave birth to me, I hope she has a husband who loves her like my dad loves my mom. And I hope she has a houseful of children. With that one decision that she made for me, she showed that she is able to put someone else first. That is the kind of quality my mom has. It's the kind of quality that *every* mom should have.

"I brought this all up because as infants and children, our parents make, or at least influence, our decisions. One mother decided to give me up for adoption because she wanted to give me a better life. And my parents decided to open their lives, home, and hearts to a child. They gave me a wonderful childhood. Those decisions were made by others and they affected the course of my life to date. But now, I'm making the decisions.

"That's what I'm here to remind you . . . we all are making our own decisions now, but those decisions impact others. We need to make the best decisions we can and be prepared to live with where those decisions lead us.

"I hope that as I start my adult life, I make decisions as good as both my mothers . . . and you too, Dad."

The audience laughed, and the camera panned to a tall, nerdy-looking man sitting next to a woman who might look plain in other circumstances, but looked absolutely stunning as she watched the daughter she loved. I remembered handing Amanda into their care all those years ago.

"That's it, I guess," Siobhan said with a smile and a shrug. "I promised you short. Go out, make decisions for your life, but as you make them, remember that each one will ripple through the rest of your life. The decision a great-great-grandmother made in another country so many years ago has rippled through generations and brought me here as much as the decisions both my mothers made. Remember, you impact the lives of others around you. So make good decisions. Congratulations again to all of us . . . and congratulations to our parents who raised us to adulthood and to the teachers who are all sighing with relief that we're out of here."

I wiped at tears even as I smiled. Siobhan had an innate sense of timing and a good sense of humor. She'd said so much in those few minutes.

I paused the DVD one last time.

"Thank you," I whispered to Ned. "I look at her and I know that my decision all those years ago was the right one. I gave her the life I wanted for her—a good life. A happy life, from the looks of it. And in return, she gave me a good life. A very happy one."

All those years of worrying. Of seeing her in the faces of the kids I helped feed. In the kids I wrote for. In the kids who were sick and afraid. I could stop seeing her in all of them.

No, no, I would still see her in every one of them because every sick, scared, hungry child could be her. Every one of them was someone's child. I would still see her in them.

I felt as if a huge weight had been lifted off me. I don't know that I ever realized how much not knowing had eaten away at me.

I felt like I could finally exhale after years of holding my breath.

It was only in its absence that I could feel the difference.

I was free.

Ned gave me those gifts. The gift of my daughter and the gift of knowing that I'd made the right decision.

For the first time since I was fifteen and told my mother I was pregnant, I could go and do anything.

I realized I didn't want to go anywhere or do anything else. Here was exactly where I wanted to be.

"So you'll wait for her to find you?" Ned asked. "I mean, I could—"

I shook my head, stopping him before he could tempt me. "When she's ready. I'll be here waiting."

He nodded.

Then I added, saying the words that Siobhan's generous speech had freed me to say, "But I hope I won't be here alone."

I'd told Anthony that I would never have any children. I'd been afraid that if my Amanda ever found me, she'd resent the children I had and kept. But that girl on the screen, the girl who was walking across the stage to collect her diploma, she wouldn't resent her half siblings. Instead, she'd said she'd be pleased, and I believed her.

And the man sitting next to me had been the one to give me the gift of my daughter.

How appropriate that the man I loved had given me my child. Not in a traditional way, but nonetheless, he had.

Ned didn't say anything, so I added, "I just want to be clear; I want to have *you* by my side."

He smiled, and I knew his answer before he said the words. "I'm glad you clarified it for me. Let me be equally clear . . . yes. If Amanda—"

"Siobhan," I corrected.

He nodded. "If Siobhan shows up tomorrow, I'll be here."

He took my hand in his. "If she shows up next year, I'll be here."

And then he kissed me.

How had I lived next to him for almost four years and not known how much I loved him?

He broke off the kiss and held me as he said, "If she doesn't show up until we're old and gray, I'll be here. I'll be sitting next to you on the front porch, watching a new crop of kids go to school."

"Watching our children and grandchildren," I said, needing him to understand that I was free.

And Ned, being Ned, did understand. He smiled and nodded. "Watching our children and grandchildren. We'll get some old-people porch rockers and we'll sit together and wait."

"What if she never comes?" I asked.

"I'll be here for you," he assured me softly. "You could try to push me away, but the harder you pushed, the faster I'd come back to you. And you need to know in your heart of hearts that I will always come back to you."

And as always, Ned was right. That's what I needed to know. But I think that maybe that's what I'd always known.

Despite my question, I knew Siobhan would come, just as I knew I would have more children. Ned's children.

"I have one more thing for you."

He went and got a piece of paper and handed it to me. It took me a moment to realize I was looking at a copy of a diploma.

"This took some work," he said.

It was a diploma made out to *Siobhan Amanda Ahearn.*

I cried again.

They'd heard me. All those years ago, her mother and father had heard me say good-bye to her and they'd made my name for her a part of her name.

They'd let me be a part of her all these years.

I cried again, but it was okay because I knew Ned would hold me. He'd be here while I cried and while I waited. I knew with no other words that he'd be here at my side.

Later, when all my tears had been shed and I'd watched the video again with Ned by my side, I said, "I love you."

"Yeah, I know," he said and laughed. "For the record, I love you, too."

I was able to laugh and say, "Yeah, you just love me *two*. But I love you *one* . . ."

Epilogue

Dear Siobhan,

I have written in this journal for four years now. I've used up almost all the pages, so this is my last entry in your book. I thought when I started writing it, I was writing it for you—as a way to tell you the story of a chapter of your life you never knew about. And in part, that's what this is. But in the end, it was the story of me as well and the stories of all the people's lives we've both touched.

Through these pages, I was trying to be your mother. All the talks we might have had, all the times I might have held you and comforted you and chased away your nightmares . . . all those and so many other mother-daughter moments I tried to wrap into these pages.

I've built my life around you, and now, as you graduate high school, like any parent, I'm letting go. There will be no empty nest for me. That came before. Now, my nest will be full. Ned and Princess live here now. And we're getting married in the fall . . . in my garden.

It's going to be a small ceremony. Just us, surrounded by family and a few friends. Coop will be there. And Jo, too.

And on that day, I'll be a wife.

It will be a new description for me.

Everyone has so many ways to describe himself or herself. We wear so many hats. I've been a daughter, a granddaughter, a student, a teacher, a nurse, a storyteller, a gardener, a . . . Every person can describe himself or herself in hundreds of ways. Reader. Writer. Cook.

Of all the ways I can describe myself, writing your book has taught me there are three designations I cherish above all.

Writer is one, not the most important one, but it's a central part of who I am. I love telling stories. I love living in other people's skins, walking in their shoes for the course of a book. I read somewhere that readers live a thousand lives. Writers live even more, and I think we live them more intimately. In some way, all of my books have let me feel a part of your life.

This fall, I'll add wife to my most cherished descriptions of myself. It seems almost superfluous because I've realized that I have loved Ned since that first day when I sat on my front porch and wrote that description of Couch Couch. I didn't realize it then, but I did. He's part of me and stands next to you in my heart.

Lastly, but always first, I am a mother. Ned was right; I've always been that. Not in the same way the mother who raised you is your mother. But in my own way. Uniquely.

I was your mother when I put your needs first and I gave you up to the parents who raised you.

I was your mother with each child I held as a nurse.

I was your mother with each child I fed through Amanda's Pantry.

I was your mother through each story I told.

I've started my next book. It's called, The Naming of Things, and the dedication for this one is different than the rest. It reads, To Siobhan . . . and Ned. You are my heart.

And in this one book are the three things I treasure most. You, Ned, and writing.

Love,
Your Other Mother
Piper

From Ned:

Dear Siobhan,
After I read the notebook and your story—Pip's story— she asked me if there was anything I wanted to add in the last few blank pages before she tucks the notebook into that trunk along with all those letters from people she's helped in your name.

I had a friend who'd seen the two of us together ask how it could have taken so long for me to realize I loved her when it was so obvious we were two halves of a whole.

I said maybe that's why.

I never bought into the idea of a soul mate—I thought it was just the tagline of romance novels. But I've changed my mind.

That day when I moved in and Pip was on her porch typing away at her computer as she drank from one of those fancy teacups she loves, she smiled at me. And in that instant, I knew that she was going to be a good neighbor.

Later, I realized she was a good friend.

And then finally, I realized that I loved her.

Why didn't I recognize that last part at first? It seems that I should have known it a lot sooner.

Josiah said it was as obvious to him as the nose on his face.

I've thought a lot about that and realized that I didn't realize it sooner because she was a part of me. Pip was a part of me before I'd even met her. So there was no shock of recognition, no moment when I thought, there she is. I've found her.

She'd always been a part of me, and when I finally realized that, I realized what that meant. She never filled a void in my life because she'd always occupied that space.

Sort of like a nose.

You have one. You see it every day in the mirror, but you've probably never really stopped and looked and thought, that is my nose. You never ask, Where would I be without it? because it's always been with you and you know that it always will be with you. You're used to seeing yourself with it. It's simply part of your reflection.

I'm pretty sure that's where the expression originated. And my loving Pip was as obvious as the nose on my face, it was harder to see because it was like a nose.

Do you follow me?

If not, don't worry. I'm not the writer in the family.

But here's what I'm saying, Siobhan. It's like that with you. I am not your birth father, nor am I the father who raised you, but you are part of me. And when you find Pip, you'll find me.

You'll find us.

And when you do, there will be no shock of recognition; there will only be a welcome home.

For wherever we are, you have a home with us . . . you are part of both of us.

And we'll be waiting for you.

~Ned

From the Author:

September 2014

Dear Reader,

I hope you enjoyed Pip and Ned's story. It's not a traditional romance. There's not some huge obstacle keeping the heroine and hero apart. And while it's as plain as . . . well, plain as the nose on your face that they're meant to be together, it takes them both some time to discover it. I think there's a truth in that kind of relationship, one that's built on a friendship that was always destined to be more, even if it took both parties some time to discover it.

As for Piper and Ned waiting for Siobhan to find them . . . I'm sure I'll hear from readers about that, so for the record, they do meet. But as Ned said, it doesn't matter when Siobhan finds them. They'll both be there, waiting for her together. And when she does find them, she'll find another home she didn't know she had.

That Ned is waiting with Pip, that he'll be there for her no matter what, is what makes this a true love story for me—the knowledge that you'll always have someone at your side through the tough times and through the joyous ones is true love.

After *Just One Thing*, my editor (the awesome Kelli Martin) and I were discussing what I would write next. We both decided that I'd try to find something that was the same but different from *Just One Thing*, which was a romance that was a little different. It was a story that walked the line between women's fiction and romance. I'm so glad I got to tell this story that's a little of both. This story of Pip, of her friendship with Ned . . . and a love that was meant to be. I hope you enjoyed it. And I hope that you'll be watching for my next same-but-different story next fall.

As always thank you to all my readers who've followed my career from romantic comedies, to romantic dramas, to comedic mysteries, and now to these new books that explore life and love from a woman's perspective. And thank you to all my new readers, too! I'm so very fortunate to have you all supporting me and cheering me on! Like Pip, there are three ways to describe me that I treasure the most. Wife, mother, and writer. Thanks for sharing part of that with me.

Holly

About the Author

Award-winning author Holly Jacobs has sold over two and a half million books worldwide. The first novel in her Everything But . . . series, *Everything But a Groom*, was named one of 2008's Best Romances by *Booklist*, and her books have been honored with countless other accolades.

Holly has a wide range of interests, from her love for writing, to gardening, and even basketweaving. She has delivered more than sixty author workshops and keynote speeches across the country. She lives in Erie, Pennsylvania, with her family and her dogs. She frequently sets stories in and around her hometown.